Belin's Hill

Also by Catherine Fisher

The Book of the Crow
The Relic Master
The Interrex
Flain's Coronet
The Margrave

Corbenic
Darkhenge
The Snow-Walker Trilogy
The Glass Tower

Belin's Hill

CATHERINE FISHER

RED FOX

BELIN'S HILL
A RED FOX BOOK 0 099 48223 1

First published in Great Britain by The Bodley Head,
an imprint of Random House Children's Books

The Bodley Head edition published 1997
First Red Fox edition published 1998
This Red Fox edition published 2005

1 3 5 7 9 10 8 6 4 2

Red Fox Books are published by Random House Children's Books,
61–63 Uxbridge Road, London W5 5SA,
a division of The Random House Group Ltd,
in Australia by Random House Australia (Pty) Ltd,
20 Alfred Street, Milsons Point, Sydney, NSW 2061, Australia,
in New Zealand by Random House New Zealand Ltd,
18 Poland Road, Glenfield, Auckland 10, New Zealand,
and in South Africa by Random House (Pty) Ltd,
Endulini, 5A Jubilee Road, Parktown 2193, South Africa

THE RANDOM HOUSE GROUP Limited Reg. No. 954009
www.kidsatrandomhouse.co.uk

A CIP catalogue record for this book is available from the British Library.

Printed and bound in Great Britain by
Cox & Wyman Ltd, Reading, Berkshire

And all alone on the hill I wondered what was true.
The White People, Arthur Machen

CHAPTER 1

With a crash, the sunlight and the street came back. The pavement beneath him was hard and hot; after a moment he tried to sit up, but he felt sick, and shaken. His sight was blurred. There was a hand on his chest, holding him down; vaguely he struggled against it. The air rang with a great roaring; car-horns, shouts, running feet. And through the hot, painful throbbing of his head he saw faces, all the faces crowding in; their nightmare whiteness, their narrow, anxious eyes.

He squirmed in fright.

Phil's voice spoke sharply behind his ear. 'Huw! Don't move! Just keep still.'

He barely heard. Somewhere at the back of the crowd, a man was watching him, a man with dark, uneasy eyes and a trickle of blood that ran slowly down his forehead. And there were trees too, black trees in a ring all around him, gnarled and bent. One of them leaned over.

'Huw?' it whispered. 'Can you speak to me, Huw?'

A wave of heat flooded him; he knew the side of his face

was burning against the hot pavement, and far away below him, deep in the earth, he heard his name called again, echoing.

Sunlight dissolved into blurs.

Into darkness.

When he opened his eyes again he realised he was indoors.

There was a dark oaken ceiling high above him, curved with garlands of leaves and fruit. A few dusty cherubs peered down, their wooden cheeks puckered into smiles. For what seemed a long time Huw lay there staring up at them, content with following the intricate twists and smooth roundness of the wood. He was lying on a long couch, against a stiff pillow that made his neck ache. Around him the room was dim, the sunlight in the windows shaded with muslin blinds. It smelt of musty old leather books, and cigarettes.

He tried to move his head. A sharp point of pain burst behind one temple and he put his hand up to it, quickly.

'Lie still!' Phil's broad face loomed over him. 'The doctor's coming.'

Huw swallowed; his mouth was dry as dust. 'Where am I?' he whispered.

Phil grinned in relief. 'I've always wanted to hear someone say that. You're at the vicarage. It was nearest.'

'Nearest to what?'

His cousin sat down, smile fading. 'To Cross Street. You nearly got hit by a car. Don't you remember?'

'I don't know.' Pictures flickered in his head. A fire. A face.

Seeing his bewilderment, Phil shrugged. 'Never mind. Lie still. We think you're all right.'

Huw lay back and stared up at the cherubs. He felt as if his mind was a box of jigsaw pieces; someone had shaken them up and nothing fitted. At last he said, 'It's a bit like the other time . . .'

'It's nothing like the other time!' Phil sounded fierce, almost angry. 'Don't think about that. This time no one's dead.' He turned in relief as the door opened.

'How is he?' a voice asked.

'Awake. A bit confused.'

The long shadow of a man moved in front of the window and paused there, against the light. As he looked up at it, another wave of dizziness swept over Huw; the figure blurred, became oddly filmy and indistinct, as if it was fading away at the edges into sunlight and the gauzy, rippling curtains. Then it stepped forward, and was the vicar, a tall, sandy-haired man, looking down at him anxiously.

'Feeling better?' he asked.

Huw shrugged, or tried to. 'My head aches. I can't remember much about what happened.'

'I'm sure that's perfectly normal.' John Mitchel sat on the edge of the sofa. 'Probably shock. You smacked your head hard on that kerb, but you were lucky. If Hal hadn't been there we might still be picking up the pieces.'

He laughed, and then the laugh went, instantly. 'Oh Huw, I'm sorry,' he murmured. 'What a stupid thing to say.'

Phil glared at him furiously.

'It doesn't matter,' Huw said stiffly.

'Of course it does. It was unforgivable.'

There was an awkward silence. Huw looked away, into the grey dusty gap between the cushions. In all his confusion, the memory of his parents' death had never gone. It stayed – a dull, heavy stone inside him. It had been three months ago. It seemed like for ever.

Gathering his thoughts with an effort he asked, 'What name did you say?'

But the vicar was on the other side of the room, at his desk. With a shock, Huw realised that a few minutes had passed.

'Hal. Hal Vaughn.' Phil came back. 'He's the man who pushed you out of the road.'

'Has he got black hair?'

'Yes. You must have seen him.'

He had seen a face somewhere. It seemed so long ago.

The vicar lit a cigarette and tossed the match down. He drew the smoke in and said, 'It was all amazingly quick. You crossed the road and the car was there. It seemed to come from nowhere . . . must have been doing sixty. Hal caught hold of you and pulled you back – you both went down.'

'How badly was he hurt?'

'Not at all, as far as I know.'

Huw looked up in surprise. 'There was blood all down his face.'

'Was there? Good Lord.' The vicar jumped up. 'In that case I'd better check he's all right. Wait here, Phil. Won't be long.'

They heard him meet someone outside; low voices echoed in the hall. Then the door banged, and Lizzie came running in.

'Where's Huw?' she gasped.

'It's all right.' Phil went towards her but she shoved him aside and came and crouched by the sofa, her face strained, her eyes wide with worry.

'It's nothing. Just a bump.' Huw insisted. He made an effort and sat up, dizzily. 'Don't get upset.'

'Upset!' She glared at him. 'Sometimes I could wring your neck.'

'Thanks,' he muttered.

Her look shocked him. She hadn't had that look for months; now he had brought it back. He knew he would have been the same; cold, numbed, then flooded by terror. After all, there were only the two of them left.

'I'm all right, Lizzie,' he said quietly. 'I just banged my head.' He swung his feet down.

She grabbed his arm. 'The doctor's here. Let him look at you first.'

He was already in the room, a small round man with glasses and a balding forehead. He wore a shirt so white it

5

gleamed, and for a moment Huw felt heat, as if flames hissed.

The doctor pulled a chair over and looked at him. 'All I can say is you must be very fond of hospitals.' He jerked his head at Lizzie and Phil. 'Outside, please.'

Reluctantly they went, Lizzie closing the door very quietly.

As he examined Huw's chest, the doctor said, 'How long since they discharged you?'

'Two weeks.' His head was tipped sideways. Desperately, he asked, 'I won't have to go back in, will I?'

'That depends. Any dizziness, flashes, ringing in your ears?'

'No,' Huw lied.

'Seeing perfectly clearly? No pain anywhere?'

'Nothing.'

A tiny torch as flashed into each eye, dazzling him. 'Walk across the room,' the doctor said, doubtfully.

Huw stood up. With a conscious effort to keep straight and casual, he walked over to the table, leaned his fingers lightly on it for a fraction of a second, and came back.

The doctor looked at him closely for a moment, then jammed the stethoscope into the bag. 'All right. No hospital. At least, not to stay. But I want you to go down and get an X-ray done, just in case.' As Huw opened his mouth, the doctor raised a hand impatiently. 'No buts, Huw. In March you fractured your skull and broke your collarbone, and they may be healed but I'm not taking any chances. Go as soon as your uncle comes. I'll ring and let them know.'

Huw nodded, bleakly. He dreaded the white corridors of the hospital, the smell of it, where each day had been endless, where he had woken every night with nightmares of the train.

'I hate that place,' he said.

The doctor gave him a sideways look. 'I'm sure you do, son.' Closing the bag he said, 'I knew your mum and dad. Met them once. Nice people.'

He was quiet a moment, watching Huw stiffly pulling his shirt back on. 'I'll give you something for headaches. You may get a few.'

Huw frowned, trying to do up his buttons. It was oddly difficult; the button and the hole wouldn't come together properly.

The doctor scribbled on the form and stood up. 'Here. You're getting a lift?'

'That's all taken care of.' The vicar came in with a tray of teacups, Lizzie and Phil behind him. 'Phil's dad is on his way.' He put the tray down and cleared some papers. 'In a bit of a state, too, at first. Had to calm him down.'

'I'm not surprised,' the doctor remarked. 'Can't stay, John. Have to go up to Ponthir . . .'

Their voices died away behind the closing door. Lizzie put down some saucers and sat by the desk, the sunlight flaming her red hair.

'Well?'

7

'Nothing. Have to have an X-ray, but it's OK.'

'More than you deserve. You scared us stiff.' Her first fear had gone, he could see. She was annoyed now. 'Didn't you see the stupid car?'

'Of course I did. That's why I stepped out.'

Phil said, 'You still look a bit white.'

'How else should I look?'

Phil grinned at Lizzie. 'Hasn't done his temper any good.' She nodded, pouring out milk. Huw knew she was still worried, but all he wanted was to get back to Phil's house – back home – and rest his head. It was aching now, throbbing hard.

'Drink this.' She gave him the tea; it was hot and strong and he was thirsty. The vicar came back and perched on the back of the sofa. He lit up a new cigarette and scratched his cheek. 'He's to go for an X-ray. Right away.'

'Don't talk about me as if I'm not here!' Huw muttered.

The room was silent a moment. Phil rattled his spoon. 'The funny thing is, tomorrow none of this could have happened.'

'Why not?'

'The excavation.'

Lizzie looked blank, so he went on.

'The people from the museum. Tomorrow they're going to dig up Cross Street. No traffic.'

The vicar shook his head. 'They're always digging somewhere. Of course the whole village is built on a huge Roman site, and maybe something older. I'm always turning up bits of pot in the garden. If it stops the traffic it will do some good.'

'What's that dark place on the hill?' Huw asked suddenly, looking up from his cup.

Lizzie stared. 'What place?'

'On the hill. Above the village.' He held the cup still, grasping for fragments of memory. 'Just before I crossed the road I was looking up there. There was a fire in the trees.'

'Belin's Hill, is it? With the hill-fort?' The vicar nodded. 'Ah yes, that's old. Belongs to Hal.' The bell on the front door jangled through the house and he stood up. 'That was quick.'

'It'll be Dad.' Phil went over to Huw. 'Are you sure you're all right now?'

'Fine.' But he was so dizzy when he stood up that only Phil's firm grip kept him upright, and for a second the dim room and its sunny windows wavered and swung around him.

The vicar came back with Huw's Uncle Tom filling the narrow doorway behind him. He said nothing, but came over and put an arm, still hot and oily from the tractor, around Huw's shoulders. 'God,' he breathed, grimly. 'This family must be accident-prone.'

Suddenly, for the first time, Huw felt his own shock rise; it became a silent sob that shook him, and he rubbed his head with his palm.

All the way down the corridor the vicar gave orders.

'X-ray. Then get him to bed. Watch the step. Right as rain in a few days.'

On the doorstep he added, 'By the way Huw, you were wrong about Hal. Sprained his wrist, but no blood. You must have imagined it.'

Huw looked back, astonished.

'No I didn't, he said.

CHAPTER 2

I t was always the same dream.

The wall of the tunnel was right up against his face, so close in the darkness that he could put out his tongue and lick the damp bricks, the salts among the ferns. Water trickled against his cheek, soaking his torn shirt. For hours he stared at the ferns; they were tiny, and pale, growing in the dark, on nothing, and behind them there was a numb, distant pain somewhere deep in his skull, and a silence full of echoes, crashing echoes that reverberated for miles down the crumpled wreckage of the train.

He could just see the corner of his mother's cardigan beside him. The wooden button was split; oil and water soaked slowly into it.

Far away, far down in the dark, beyond the shards of glass and the smoke, was an arch of sunlight. As he watched it someone came and stood there, looking in. A man, tiny in the distance. For a moment he was still. Then he was running towards Huw, but slowly – as if in some nightmarish slowed-down film, blurring in and out of

11

focus. Huw struggled to get up, but his chest was pinned by a heavy weight. When he coughed his mouth was full of dust.

He was scared. It was always the same dream, but this time something was wrong, something was different. He felt it, it began to move in the earth under his trapped fingers, something hard, forcing its way up. Soil crumbled, stones rattled and fell; he felt the shape uncovering, something smooth, round, cold as stone.

His fingers felt a forehead.

A mouth.

Huw sat bolt upright in the bed.

Sweat was running down his back; he was breathing fast; he looked round, astonished. Sunlight dappled the flowered wallpaper of the room and somewhere outside the tractor started up and went rolling down the track, its tyres crunching over stones.

He put his arms round himself and rocked back and forth, slowly.

'Are you awake?' His aunt knocked on the door.

He sat rigid. 'Yes.'

'Decent?'

'In bed.'

She put her head round the door, letting the scent of coffee into the room. 'Breakfast's ready.' Then she stepped in, her arms full of clothes. 'You look washed out, Huw.'

He nibbled the corner of the quilt. 'A bit.'

'I could fetch up a tray. Special treat.'

'No. I'll get up now. I'm fine.'

She nodded, but didn't move, looking thoughtfully round the attic. 'We'll get this re-decorated for you. Something a bit more suitable. And Tom can put up some shelves for your books and models. It's always been the spare room. Hasn't been touched for years.'

He nodded, feeling the sweat cool on his back. Lizzie's laugh came from downstairs, and Phil's deeper voice. His aunt pushed a curl of blonde hair from her eyes and said, quietly, 'We're very glad to have you both here. You do know that, don't you?'

'Yes,' he said, and lay back on the pillow.

She stood there a moment as if she was waiting for something else. Then she went downstairs.

Listening to her footsteps, Huw tried to remember what had happened in the dream, but the memory was already gone. It had been different; not just the usual horror of the crumpled train. He drew his knees up under the sheet, hugging them.

It was warm, and quiet. He looked around.

The room was smaller than his old one at home; the roof sloped down to a window with a deep sill in the wall opposite, the leaves of the apple-tree rustling against it. His belongings were piled carefully around the bare walls, for him to arrange as he wanted. Up till now, he'd avoided doing it. He had often stayed here on holiday – it wasn't strange to him – but the idea that it was home now, that he and Lizzie were living here for good, sent a tiny start of fear through his heart. The train crash had changed the world. Instantly.

His old house . . . but he didn't want to think about that. Instead, he slid out of bed and padded over to the window, letting it swing open. The day was already hot. Beyond the orchard trees he could see the hill with the fortress on. Belin's Hill. It was dark, as if under cloud-shadow; a brooding mass of trees and ridges that squatted on the crest. It had begun to fascinate him. Lying in bed all day yesterday it had drawn his eyes, constantly; finally he had tossed his book aside and just stared at it, framed in the blue window, and the desire had grown in him to climb up there, where it would be cool, and shady. Thoughtfully he turned away, and dressed.

After breakfast Lizzie pushed the fat, ginger cat from her lap. 'So what shops, then?'

'In Caerleon. I just need a few things,' her aunt said.

Phil groaned, but his mother ignored him. 'I'll give you a list. The walk will do you good.'

Their uncle was at the sink, soaping tractor oil up his hairy arms. 'Keep Huw on the pavement,' he muttered, grinning.

No one else smiled. His wife glared at him.

Caerleon was a quarter of a mile through the lanes, the high hedgerows pale with dust. Trailing behind the others in the heat, Huw felt as if he was seeing the place for the first time, as if his sight had somehow been splintered, sharpened, put back together. The village was old; a place of layers, one below another, and the one he lived in was at the top, with its cars and satellite dishes. But even here the houses seemed to have sprouted from some deeper time, jammed together, jutting into the street, or vanishing at the end of long gardens.

The shops, some of them, lived in two layers at once. Like the chemist's – its bow window full of toothpaste boxes, and the date 1759 painted over the door.

They bought some ice-creams, and sat down to eat them.

The castle was one ruined tower in a pub car-park, where tourists' children climbed. The walls were baking in the heat; leaning back, Huw thought that under him, in the deepest levels, was a time far more remote, a place of soil and burial and worm-tunnels, of coins and lost faces.

Faces.

The word caught him; he sucked the end of the ice-cream off the stick and saw for a brief instant the shadow of a face, dark, its eyes narrow.

He tossed the stick down. 'Have we got everything?'

'More or less.' Phil tugged the list from his pocket and looked at it lazily. 'Except her shampoo. They haven't got it.'

'Take her another sort,' Lizzie said.

'What?' Phil rolled over on the grass, closing his eyes. 'She's too fussy!'

'Tired?' Lizzie teased.

'It's all right for you,' he mumbled. 'I have to get up and feed the hens. And Huw spent yesterday in bed.'

'Let's climb up there,' Huw said abruptly.

They both stared at him.

'Where?'

'The hill-fort.' He was gazing up at it, the dark distant trees moving as if in a breeze.

'It's too hot,' Lizzie groaned.

'And I've got this stuff to carry,' Phil sat up. 'Another time, Huw. We'd better get back.'

But Huw didn't move. He sat, knees drawn up, his back against the warm wall. 'I'm going up,' he said.

Something in his voice made them stop and look at him; he looked strained and tense, his fingers gripped tight.

Lizzie stared curiously up at the hill. 'What on earth for?'

'Just to go. To climb up.' There was more, but he didn't know how to say it.

'Tomorrow, Huw,' Phil said firmly. But Huw was already on his feet; he strode off up the street between the cars and the white glare of the cottages. 'Go home if you want,' he called back, bitterly. 'I can find the way.'

They gazed after him. 'It's miles,' Phil groaned.

'We'd better go after him. He's not supposed to do anything too strenuous.' Lizzie glanced at Phil. 'He's been different lately.'

'Hardly surprising.' Phil heaved the carrier bag under one arm. 'Not after all that's happened.'

'It happened to me, too.'

He looked at her, and said gently, 'I know, Liz. But he was there; he was in that train. It must have been terrible.'

She nodded. 'Not being there is pretty bad too.'

Phil didn't know what to say, but she smiled up at him. 'Come on, let's stay with him. He'll wear himself out.' She started down the street, quickly.

It took them at least an hour to climb the hill in the glaring heat, and they were all tired and thirsty and irritable by the time they reached the lowest rampart. Phil opened a bottle of Coke and they all drank some, but it was warm and too fizzy, shaken up in the bag under his arm. 'We must be mad,' he muttered, wiping sweat from his hair.

Lizzie sprawled on the grass, biting a stem. Clouds of seed drifted up around her; ladybirds crawled red among the ferns. The hill crackled with heat; its dry growth crisp, the soil among the roots warm to touch. Above them the sky was a blue unbroken dome.

Huw was too impatient to lie there long. As soon as he had his breath back he got up quietly and climbed on, the rampart towering above him. Sweating, his head throbbing strangely with the effort, he attacked the slope. Bees hummed around him in the shimmering air; nettles and brambles loaded with unripe berries scratched his bare arms as he struggled up, snapping the long stems of fox-gloves, seed in his hair.

At the top was a slight ditch full of bracken, then another bank, and a third, until Huw hauled himself up on weary arms he could see the long swell of other lands below, strange to him; a web of fields in the bowl of the valley, all the villages and lanes to Usk, and the dark ridge of Wentwood against the sky.

There was a breeze up here; a cool wind. He pulled off his soaked shirt and flung it down; the air was cold on his body and he stretched, suddenly happy. Below was the village, the muddy river winding through it like a snake, the hum of cars loud on its bridge.

'Huw? Where are you?' It was Lizzie's shout, sounding anxious.

'At the top,' he said.

And it was then, sharp as a spear, that the pain struck him. Astonishing, like a crack of lightning, the spasm jerked through his skull; his sight became a nauseous blur. He caught his breath, teeth clenched, found his hands pressing hard against his face, squeezing in the vice of pain till water gathered in his eyes and under his fingers. He took deep, shuddering breaths. This was unbearable, worse than all the headaches in the hospital; he wanted to shout, to scream for Lizzie, but his voice was choked, and yet he found he could see, though the hilltop was nothing but a green, shimmering haze. And in the ripple of heat someone was standing: someone tall, blurred, his face

18

tattooed with whirling lines, his eyes narrow and fierce. Greens of the wood stained him over; he was a patchwork of browns and mud-splash, leaves and feathers, a scatter of pierced bones that clattered from his belt, and as he opened his scarred lips the words were a bitter hiss like the crackle of flame.

Huw scrambled back, tingling with pain.

The figure stepped closer, its outline rippling, dappled with shadows, so close to him he could smell the rankness of it, the damp smell of stirred earth.

Then it put out a hand, and caught hold of him.

CHAPTER 3

'Sit down. It'll pass.'

The hill was silent, but for the voice and the stir of branches. Then, slowly, as if from a great distance, the hum of the traffic swung back. Huw's sight cleared. The pain ebbed. He wiped water from his eyes.

The man wore a green pullover, spattered with mud and frayed at the sleeves. He was watching Huw closely, his eyes dark and narrow. A small black spaniel sat behind him on the grass, panting.

'I think you should get out of the sun,' the man said. His voice was cool, with an odd undertone of anxiety.

Huw stood up, dragging in breath. He was unsteady and his skull tingled; he felt foolish. 'I'm fine, thanks,' he said, resentfully.

'So what was it?' Still crouched, the stranger looked up at him intently. 'What did you see?'

'Sorry?'

'You saw something, didn't you? Something that scared you.'

For a moment Huw stared at the man, at his narrow, familiar face. 'The sun was in my eyes,' he mumbled.

The man was still. Then he stood up.

'For heaven's sake, Huw!' Lizzie's voice said irritably. 'Couldn't you have found a better path than this?'

Her hair appeared first, red and tangled; then her scratched arms as she hauled herself up, and flung a spider off her shoulder.

'Look at the legs on that!'

'No need to be personal.' Phil scrambled up beside her, breathless, and they both giggled. She stopped when she saw Huw. 'What's the matter?'

'Nothing. I'm all right.' He was aware of the silent man watching them; the others stood slowly as they noticed him.

'This is private land,' he said. Huw saw his mood had changed. The concern was gone. Now there was something about him that they all felt to be disturbing: a guarded hostility.

Then Lizzie noticed the strapping on his wrist, and realised who he was.

'Sorry, Mr Vaughn,' Phil said, shifting the carrier bag under his arm. 'My fault.'

The man glanced at him. As if with an effort, he said, 'That's all right, Phil.'

There was an awkward silence.

Lizzie rubbed the dog's silky ears. As it snuffled round her shoes, she glanced at Huw who was glaring at the grass and said, 'We haven't thanked you for what you did for my brother the other day. The vicar said he might have been killed.'

Hal Vaughn shrugged. 'The vicar often exaggerates.'

He was younger than she'd thought, from that glimpse in the street. She felt he had steeled himself against her words, as if they were some ordeal.

'Still, I mean it.'

And she was right, because he said, 'Thank you' gravely.

Triumphant, she rubbed the dog's ears.

Hal turned away. 'Come on, Mick!' The dog ran to him and he brushed through the long grass to a gap in the rampart.

'Wait . . . wait a minute!'

Huw looked up. Lizzie raised her eyebrows. It was about time he had some manners.

But when Huw spoke the words came out in a rush. 'Was there a fire up here that day?'

Lizzie stared at him in astonishment.

Hal turned. He seemed amazed, then wary. 'What day?'

'Friday. When you . . . when the car nearly hit us. I was looking up here, I remember. There was a fire, a big one. The smoke was going up in a black column.'

For a moment Hal was very still. Then he said, 'There's been no fire up here. Not for a long time.'

'But I saw it!'

'No.'

Huw stared at him, furious, but the man stared back, eyes dark in the sunlight. 'You must have been mistaken.'

'I wasn't!'

Hal shrugged. 'Show me the scorch marks then. I'm up here most days. I would have seen it.'

Bewildered, Huw gazed around. Nettles and bracken rose like a sea about his knees, a thicket of oak trees dark behind him. There was no mark of any fire.

'Through those trees,' he snapped.

Hal gave one quick glance at Lizzie and Phil. Embarrassed now, Lizzie muttered. 'You might have imagined it . . .'

'No!' Huw rounded on her, hotly. 'I'm not seeing things. It was real.' He turned and marched away from them between the oaks, angry with all of them. He wasn't seeing things! He wasn't.

The branches of the oaks were tangled and gnarled; he forced his way among them fiercely, ignoring the scratches of the thin briars that whipped back and stung his face. Mosses coated the bark and the meshed branches; the green gloom smelt mustily of earth, of the young tender shoots of bracken that broke and cracked under his feet. He didn't care if the others were following, or if he was trespassing, or what Vaughn did about it. He needed to know that he hadn't imagined the fire.

Crashing through the undergrowth, he stumbled through a bank of ferns, abruptly, into sunlight.

The inner ring of the hillfort was surrounded by trees,

dark and gnarled. Here the hot air shimmered, unmoving; far overhead one wisp of cloud barely drifted. Long grass covered humps and hollows, strange irregularities in the soil. Out in the centre, one stone pillar leaned in the heat.

'Well?' Hal had come out of the thicket, with the dog running behind him. He came up to Huw and said urgently, 'Where was the fire then?' Shadows dappled his face with greens and browns.

Hot, confused, Huw shook his head. 'You know it was here,' he said bitterly. 'You must have seen it. Why don't you tell them? Do you want them to think I'm mad?'

Hal winced. A brief flicker passed over his face, a glimpse of some memory; then it was gone.

He rubbed his forehead. 'Something's happened to you,' he murmured. 'You know that, don't you? To both of us. In that split-second in the street.'

For a moment they both stared at each other, as Lizzie and Phil pushed through and untangled themselves and stood breathless on the hill-top. No one mentioned the fire. Lizzie wanted to get Huw's mind off it; she was getting more worried about him.

'What's that?' she asked, pointing to the stone.

'Take a look,' Hal said dryly. 'Now you're here.'

Grass to her knees, she walked over. Huw trailed behind.

The pillar of stone was taller than Lizzie. It leaned to one side, blotched and mottled by overlapping splotches of lichen, powder-green and grey. On the top was a cavity:

a hollow bowl smoothed by rain. Lizzie touched it.

'Something went in there. How old is this?'

'As old as the fort,' Hal said, from behind.

'A thousand years?'

'More like two.'

'All that time!' Her fingers stroked the granite; a few tiny grains of it rolled like sand into the grass.

Huw looked round. There was no scorching; no blackened circles of charcoal. Angrily he reached out and touched the stone, jerking his hand back so suddenly that Hal noticed.

'Hot?' he asked quietly.

Huw turned away, clenching his burnt fingers.

CHAPTER 4

The vicar always liked to know what was going on. It was part of his delight in spicing up his sermons with local gossip, and watching people in church open their eyes, astonished. Now he stuck stamps on his letters outside the Post Office, and waved at Phil and Lizzie.

'Come and look at this.'

Cross Street was empty of traffic, railed off with orange police tape that fluttered across the road. A large red diversion sign pointed past The Bull Inn. Already the dig was underway.

'It's just where Huw fell down,' Lizzie murmured, running over.

'So it is. How are you both? Settling in?'

She shrugged. 'Yes, thanks.'

The vicar nodded. He'd seen Tom Griffiths yesterday; he knew Huw wasn't settling. 'Miles away,' Phil's father had said, worried. 'As if he can't take in what happened, as if he won't think about it or touch it, as if it's some burned, sore place in his memory.'

Remembering it, the vicar said, 'Where is he, by the way?'

'In the shop.'

Mitchel looked back and saw Huw come out of the Post Office and stand on the kerb, waiting to cross. He looked pale. 'I'll tell you what,' he said quietly to Lizzie, 'I think your brother needs something to do.'

'To do?'

'Yes. I know it's the holidays, but hanging around and doing nothing is just the way for him to brood on things – about the train, and your parents I mean. Take my advice, Lizzie. Find something to occupy him.'

Phil called. Huw waved and stepped off the kerb, and each of them felt a memory of sudden fear stab them, the flash of the red car in its flurry of dust.

Huw seemed to be thinking of it too. When he spoke his voice was subdued. 'What's going on?'

'They're excavating. Remember?'

The clink of trowels and shovels was the only sound in the heat. Dropping his last letter in the box, the vicar led them closer, curious, lighting a cigarette, one hand cupped around the match flame.

They saw that the road surface had been drilled away. A long trench had been opened right down the street, and about six or seven students in shorts and T-shirts and old hats were chipping cautiously away at the sub-soil, each bent in their dreamy huddle. Metal pegs stuck out of the sides of the trench, each with a fluttering fragment of white paper. Mitchel bent over and read one. It said 40/201. A trickle of soil slid from under his shoe into the trench.

'Hey! Be careful . . . please.' A girl glared at him over the top of a large drawing board.

'Sorry! Sorry!' He raised a hand in apology, and muttered. 'What did I do?'

Phil grinned, shaking his head. Only Huw had seen the earth slither down. He stared at it, silent. It reminded him of something, but he couldn't think what.

'A bit hot down there in the pits of hell?' the vicar remarked, genially.

'A bit.'

'And what exactly are you looking for? Romans?'

The girl sharpened her pencil patiently. She wore a baggy shirt and beads, and cut-off shorts. 'I can see we're going to have to put some sort of notice up,' she muttered to the digger next to her.

Looking up she said, 'Not Romans, not this time. We're going deeper. We want to see what was here before the Romans built their fortress. Right back, into the dark.' Huw stared into the trench. There was a man digging just below him. He watched, fascinated, as the small trowel cut slices out of the dry soil, crumbling it away, revealing worm-holes and grit and pebbles and lumps of congealed earth that the man picked over with his fingers. Some he threw back; others were tossed into a rusty finds tray. They all looked the same to Huw. The digger brushed the soil into a hand shovel and tipped it into a bucket. He emptied that onto a heap outside the trench. Then he stood and stretched and grinned at them.

'Got a light?'

John Mitchel tossed him a box of matches. 'So what was here?'

'We're not sure yet. It looks like some sort of religious site. A ritual sanctuary.' He winked and gave the matches back. 'Blood and death and strange gods.'

'Right up my street,' the vicar laughed.

Lizzie groaned; Phil touched her arm. 'Look who's here.'

Looking up, she saw Hal Vaughn standing near them on the pavement, the spaniel scratching at the soil.

'Fine morning, Hal,' the vicar said.

Hal said nothing, but nodded, glancing at them all.

'This one's back on his feet,' the vicar explained.

Hal gave Huw a rapid look. 'I know. We met yesterday.'

'Oh?'

'On Belin's Hill,' Lizzie put in.

'Ah.' The vicar opened a paper bag and began to pick out plums from a box outside the grocers. 'Huw's idea?'

Huw scowled; Lizzie nodded, sweeping her long hair back in one hand. 'It was quite interesting too. There's a stone pillar up there . . .'

The digger looked up from his trowel. 'Is there? I didn't know that.'

'It's private land,' the vicar said, giving Hal a quick glance.

'So keep off,' Hal said, curtly. The digger shrugged.

The vicar waved a plum at the excavation. 'So what do you think of it all?'

'You know what I think.' Hal's voice was bitter, so that they all looked at him. 'I hate it.'

'Why?' Lizzie asked, quietly.

He glanced at her. 'Some things should be left alone.'

In the heat the trowels clinked; cars flashed along the road. A small point of pain began to nag at Huw's forehead. He rubbed it, absently.

'People have to find out –' Phil began, but Hal interrupted him, his hands clenched on the wooden rail.

'Do they?' He glanced down into the pit. 'How can they? They only find objects. They won't find out how those people thought, what they believed; all their terrors, what they feared in the dark. Where's that buried? Down there? Or is that buried in us?'

The vicar stopped picking plums. 'Race memory? That's interesting.'

Phil shrugged. 'It still doesn't hurt to dig things up.'

Hal looked at him, a strange, sharp look. 'It's dangerous. Dragging things to the light.'

The girl with the drawing board had been listening. She said 'There's nothing down here but bits of old pot.'

Hal shook his head. He looked tense and bitter. 'The past is down there.'

'We can't bring that back!' she laughed.

'How do you know?' Hal stepped back, his eyes dark. 'How do you know?'

'So you think the dig should be stopped?' Lizzie said, quietly.

'Yes. Stopped, destroyed, closed down.' He was shaking, Huw saw with surprise. Several passers-by turned to look at them all, as if they had heard.

Mitchel put the last plum thoughtfully in the paper bag. Then he said, 'Hal . . . have you thought any more about what I asked?'

Hal stared at him. 'What?'

'You remember. About letting me have Henllys, for the concert.'

Something in Hal seemed to shut down, instantly. 'I don't think so, John.'

'Ah, but look –'

'No. I'd rather not.'

The vicar shook his head, ruefully. 'Give me time. I'll persuade you.'

Hal laughed. 'If anyone could, it would be you.' He took another dark look at the excavation, called the dog, and walked into the High Street.

'Now there's a man who lives too much alone,' the vicar said softly, cradling the plums. 'Up there in that decaying old house.'

Lizzie smiled. 'Do you know everyone's problems?'

'Indeed I do. And I give them all excellent advice. The

31

trouble is, no one listens to it. Wait there!' He vanished into the shop.

Phil grinned, kicking the kerb. 'He's a real case.'

Huw looked at him. 'Who is that man Vaughn?'

'Lives up at Henllys.' Phil leaned his back against the warm brick wall. 'It was a manor house once, but it's falling down. I've never been in. Not many people have.'

'Is he rich?'

Phil laughed. 'You must be joking. He makes pottery and sells it. They used to be, once. They've had a strange history, that family.' He straightened. 'I'll show you something.'

When the vicar came out, he said, 'Can we go in the church? Just for a minute?'

'It's always open!'

The streets were hot, and empty. The church clock clicked and whirred as they approached it, and three low chimes seemed to float out and hang, echoing, in the sun. A few old men came out of The White Hart, blinking in the glare. The pub door closed behind them.

'Rush hour,' Phil said.

The vicar grinned.

Walking along the kerb, trying to keep his balance, Huw's foot jolted into the gutter, for the second time. Standing in the sun at the dig had made him dizzy; he rubbed his head, irritably. There was nothing wrong with him. Just the heat. And that trickle of soil.

The church door opened with an echo like thunder

rumbling. It was very cool inside: the cool of marble and stone. Huw felt the sweat chill between his shoulders as he walked up the aisle. Soft blurs of light from the stained-glass fell on benches and the distant effigies of knights.

'The Vaughn chapel,' Phil said. 'Come and see.'

He led them by benches smelling of polish, hymn books with tattered corners. Carved plaques covered the walls, and large grey stones were embedded all down the aisle, worn flat by centuries of feet. Georgian Vaughns, Elizabethan Vaughns; Henry, Thomas, Eliza, Ann, the same names recurring, century after century. Beloved husband, devoted wife, daughters, brothers, sons. The newest was a small slate slab with the date 1983 and the inscription 'THOMAS VAUGHN. REST IN PEACE.'

'Hal's father.' Phil looked at the bunch of pale roses beside it. 'Died in some sort of institution.'

Lizzie stared. 'He was mad?'

'Mental illness. I don't know what, really.'

Shocked, they let the whisper drift through the church, staring down at the stark inscription. Huw stayed after the others had wandered away, remembering Hal's anger at the excavation. Things buried inside us, he had said. Dangerous things.

'Huw? Come and see this.' Lizzie sounded sarcastic. 'You'll be interested.'

They were standing before a window; it was small and perfectly round. Pictured on it in apple-green glass was Belin's Hill, the ramparts and the trees dark against a pure blue sky. The hill was pieced together from greens and browns, except for one bright red piece, near the top. Underneath, like a picture from an old book, was Caerleon, with its stiff red roofs, and the church, and all around, in the glass, were letters. Tilting his head, Huw read them.

'ROWENA VAUGHN ANNO DOMINI 1609. FOR THAT SHE HATH NO GRAVE.'

'Why not?' Lizzie asked, reaching up to touch it.

'Because she was burned.' The vicar came up behind them, took out a cigarette, remembered where he was and put it away. 'Terrible story. She was tried for witchcraft and found guilty. Her sons were the chief witnesses against her.'

'Her own family?' Lizzie was aghast.

'Well, yes. It happens. And the legend says – there's always one – that she cursed the Vaughns to the end of their race.' He scratched his ear. 'Odd thing is, there's a lot of people who'd say that came true. Many of them died strangely. And they used to own everything. Now Hal just has Henllys, which is falling down.'

'Burning people is barbaric,' Lizzie muttered, quite angry.

'Was. We don't still do it, do we?'

'Why is there a red piece in the glass?' Huw asked suddenly.

The vicar looked at him. 'Good question. No one's quite sure. The vicar before me had a theory it was a patch. But I'll tell you what the old folks say. They say Rowena Vaughn was burned on Belin's Hill, and that,' he touched it with his yellow-stained finger, 'that's the fire.'

CHAPTER 5

Huw was an archaeologist, kneeling on the cool, damp soil. His hands were muddy; the knees of his pyjamas sodden. The small trowel made his palm hot and sore as he dug with it, scraping and scratching at the rich brown earth of the trench; he was hot, and thirsty, and his shoulder muscles ached. Trees overhung him; looking up he saw that they were springing out around him from the pavement of Cross Street, cracking and splintering the stones, forcing themselves up. Leaves flapped against the light from the lampposts; moths moved about him noiselessly, brushing his face and forehead.

Then the trowel struck something hard.

The jolt woke him. Opening his eyes, he saw the bedroom was dark, and only the faint hands on his clock glowed. Five to three. As he looked at them they began to spin, slowly, backwards, and he wasn't surprised. Leaves tapped at the window. A candle on the sill lit itself with a faint plip, the flame stretching, long and smoky in the warm night.

He was still dreaming after all. So it didn't matter that he got out of bed, tugged his shoes on and crept silently downstairs.

The hall of the farmhouse was draughty and smelt of toast. He took his denim jacket from the hook by the mirror and pulled it on. Unlatching the door, he stepped outside.

The night was warm, sweet with the scents of flowers; roses and stock and lavender from the garden behind the house. The trees on the rise over the fields were dark against the deep purple sky, the breeze barely stirring them.

He crossed the yard, quickly. The old dog watched him pass, silent, nose on paws. As he tugged the gate open it creaked, and he glanced back in fear at the farmhouse, and saw in the candle-bright window of his room a face, a narrow face, watching him. He waved at himself, and slipped out.

Then he was running; running down the dim lanes, into the tunnels the hedges made. Only the narrow strip of sky was pale, and the gleam of stones on the track, and far ahead, as he turned a corner, a few early lights in the windows of the village. He ran faster, his footsteps pattering in the stillness, the sweat gathering down his back, soaking his scalp. I'm coming, he gasped, between breaths. Wait for me. I'm coming.

Breathless, he flung himself round a bend, and the night cracked open into light; two huge lights like owl-eyes, sweeping up, over him, dazzling him. A soft roar brushed him, the screech of a gear-change. Then the car had passed, purring up the hill.

Half in the hedge, Huw stood rigid.

After a moment, reaching out, he caught hold of a bramble and squeezed it, feeling the sharp stab of the thorns, the hard, unripe berries in his fist. He stared at the lane in disbelief.

What on earth was he doing? Why had he come out here? A sense of frantic hurry was fading from his mind, the memory of words . . . he grasped after them but they were gone, and he was awake. This was no dream, it was real; he could feel the dew soaking his ankles. Was he going mad?

He knew suddenly what the driver must have glimpsed; a thin boy in pyjamas and a jacket, dazzled against the hedge. Turning, he saw the car had stopped; its tail-lights flashed red. Then, quickly, it began to back down towards him, the engine whining high.

Huw ran. He came to a gate and climbed over, his feet sliding on the damp steel tubes.

'Hello?' A man's voice called from the open car door. 'Hey! Are you lost? Are you all right?'

Huw could just see him above the hedge; the shadow of his head turning. Huddled in the dark, deep among nettles and something with a sweet, sickly stink, he gathered his breath, hands clutched.

What a stupid, stupid thing to do! He was half-tempted

to get up, to speak, to tell the man that he was all right, that he had just come out for a walk, but he couldn't, not now. His head had begun to ache, and he was so tired, and the dizziness he dreaded seemed to sweep over him, softly, all at once.

'Go away!' he whispered fiercely, putting his head down on his hands. 'Just get lost!'

A footstep in the lane silenced him. The man had come to the gate and was leaning over it, his bulk dark against the pale sky.

'Is anyone there?' he said, his voice low. Then, 'I won't hurt you. I could drive you home.'

Huw sat still, breath held, peering between nettles. A moth brushed his face, its furry wing soft.

The man waited. He put his foot on the bar and, for a despairing moment, Huw thought he would climb over, but an owl hooted eerily in the woods behind, and the man turned back. His footsteps were loud in the empty lane.

It seemed an age before the car door slammed.

Then the engine started, shattering the night, and the car drove off, fading away slowly, leaving him in a sudden, appalling silence. Carefully, he stood up. The muscles of his shoulders were knotted with tension; sweat chilled on his back.

As he stood there listening he heard the tree tops swish far above him, and he knew the car had gone and he was alone out here. He was afraid too. Not of the night, the sounds of darkness, but of himself. What had made him come out here? Why hadn't he realised what he was doing? Rubbing the nettle-stings with his fingers he went back wearily and climbed the gate, looking down at the lights of Caerleon.

Wait for me.

The words came back, and he murmured them, bewildered.

A cow coughed, making his heart leap with terror. Turning, he saw the dim shapes of the herd ambling towards him through the dark, their tails swishing the long grass. They crowded against the gate, tongues rasping the bars; one mooed loudly.

'Get off!' He jumped down and walked hurriedly up the lane, hot and irritable and tense. By the time he reached the farm gate the sky was pink in the east; he knew Uncle Tom would be up soon, so he dumped his coat and ran noiselessly up to the attic, closing his door and letting out his breath in a long gasp of relief.

The room was dark; the candle unlit. The clock hands said four thirty. He climbed onto the tumbled sheets and lay there, staring at the dim ceiling, letting the sweat dry on him, trying to control the small icy throb of terror deep in his stomach.

He must have walked in his sleep. He had never done it before. And it hadn't been like sleep; he could remember what he had done but not why; only that it had been urgent, that he had been going somewhere definite. He thought about that moment on Belin's Hill; the flash of pain, the blurred image of a man, a scarred, tattooed man. But that was nothing. The pain had caused that, and the sun; headaches were one of the after-effects, they had warned him of that in the hospital. Maybe sleep-walking was too.

He turned over, convincing himself, arguing, talking his fears down. When the sun rose, he was finally asleep.

Lizzie woke him, bouncing on the bed, plaiting her hair into an elastic band.

'You look terrible.'

'So do you.' He curled up, crossly. 'Go away, Liz.'

'Can't. It's half past nine and I think you ought to get up. You're not at home now, Huw.'

He rolled over and glared at her. She shrugged, rather wan. 'Yes, I know. This is home. But you know what I mean . . .'

'No, I don't! We're not visitors. We live here. We don't have to be on our best behaviour all the time!'

She crossed to the window and unlatched it, looking out. A bee hummed in, buzzing against the panes, and the sunlight lit the fringes of her hair. He couldn't see her face.

'It's hard, isn't it?' she said after a while.

He swung his legs out and sat on the edge of the bed. 'A bit.'

They were silent, hearing the noises of the farm; the clatter of dishes in the kitchen, voices, Phil's radio. Huw thought suddenly about home, his mother calling him up the stairs, the smell of the rooms, the creak of the floorboard on the landing, the rattle of the doorhandle, a sound so familiar he could hear it now, inside his head, perfectly.

'Do you ever think about them?' he asked, softly.

He heard her turn, felt the surprise in her. 'All the time. Don't you?'

'Sometimes.' But when he closed his eyes it was the dark wall of the tunnel he saw, and the tiny ferns.

Lizzie stirred. 'Anyway, get up. We're going up to Henllys.'

He looked at her, and the shadow of Belin's Hill behind her. 'Vaughn's house? What for?'

'Because I want to. He makes pots. Aunty Ffion's birthday is on Saturday. I might buy her one.'

Huw nodded. 'And because you're nosey.'

She grinned. 'Very.'

Thinking of the fire he had seen on the hill, he pulled his socks on, quickly. 'So am I,' he muttered.

CHAPTER 6

Lizzie had been fascinated by the story of Rowena Vaughn. Watching the boys far ahead, pushing each other into the hedge, she imagined the woman climbing Belin's Hill in the early morning, how the dew would soak her long red skirts. And had they been there, at the fire, her sons? Had they stayed and watched the flames leap up? Or had they been somewhere else, as she, Lizzie, had been? It still hurt; she still felt guilty, as if, if she had been in that train, she could have done something. She shrugged. Died, probably. It was stupid to think like that.

She kicked a pebble, thinking of a whole family under a curse. They must have been sorry after. That's why the window was in the church.

'Come on, dreamer!'

Phil was waiting for her where the lane turned, Huw idling on ahead. She smiled at him. She knew how sorry he felt for them both; how hard he was trying. Not easy, to have two new people in the family, all at once.

43

They walked on through a grey-blue morning. Veils of soft haze hung over the countryside, misting the hills; some clumps of trees on the far skyline were so faint that they might have been washed in with water-colour. Before them the great crest of Belin's rose up like a threatening mass, its dark tree line indistinct.

Here in the deep lane the tarmac was warm. Tall hemlocks swayed in the ditches, their woody stems tangled with cobwebs. Phil shaded his eyes and watched the sun's long beams swirling the river haze to cloudy gold.

'Another hot day. We haven't had rain for weeks. Not since you came, really.'

Yawning, she nodded. Far ahead Huw swished the foxgloves with a stick. The lane was long and deeply rutted. It passed between two high gateposts smothered with ivy, and then climbed again, into a smooth curve.

Lizzie took off her cardigan, knotting it round her waist. Huw called, waving them on. When they reached him they saw, round the bend, that they were high above the valley; it lay below them in swirls of mist, shimmering over the fields. And looking down on it was the house.

It was very old. Ivy strangled its slate-blue stones, so that its shape was a mystery. Coming closer they saw gables jutting out in odd places. There were turrets, arched doors, tiny mysterious windows half-hidden in corners. The roof was layered with slabs of slate, crusted with mustard-yellow lichen, and swollen in places by damp, bushes sprouting from the chimneystacks.

'I see what you mean,' Lizzie said quietly.

Phil nodded. 'Ramshackle. Let's try round the front.'

Overawed, they made their way round in silence. The great manor seemed deserted; the hush of decay hung round it. Here the windows were larger, emblazoned with dim shields looking down on the valley.

A porch led to the door, and next to that an arch into a small courtyard, overgrown by a bush of dark crimson roses. Weeds grew everywhere, from cracks and crevices. Waist-high grasses lapped the downstairs windows like a wild green sea.

There was no bell on the door, so Phil opened it carefully and listened. The porch smelled of damp.

'Hello! Anyone in?'

Lizzie jerked at his sudden shout. Echoes rang in the house but no one came.

'He's out.' Huw was oddly relieved.

Phil pulled a face. 'Maybe. Or in the outbuildings.'

'It's a strange house,' Lizzie said, thoughtfully. She trampled through the long grass to a downstairs window. Huw followed, looking in, shading the glare from his eyes. He saw a long, low hall, panelled with wood. It was empty of furniture.

Barking broke out so suddenly behind them that he jumped, and as he spun around the black spaniel hurtled round the corner of the building and stood stockstill.

Then it growled again, furiously, and a flock of rooks flapped cawing out of the trees.

'Quiet, Mick!' Hal dropped some sacks against the wall and came towards them, sweeping the dog up in his arms, its pink tongue flickering between his fingers.

'He's fierce,' Phil remarked.

'Not really.' Hal looked at them all. 'You seem very fond of my property.'

They were silent, unsure. Then Lizzie said, 'Yes, but this time it's business.'

'What business?'

'Pottery. I want to buy some. It's Phil's mother's birthday,' she added, lamely.

'I see.' Hal put the dog down and it ran towards her, so she bent and rubbed its smooth back. Then Hal said, 'But I supply the craft centre, and that's nearer. Why not go there?'

'I thought you might be cheaper.' She smiled at him, and after a moment he smiled back, ruefully. They all knew he didn't believe her.

'I see,' he said again. 'Wait here a minute.' He went into the house.

'You've got a nerve,' Phil muttered.

'Why?'

'Coming out with it like that. You never know with him – he's got a bit of a temper. He knows you're here just to nose around.'

Lizzie glared at him. 'So are you!'

46

'Me? I'm just keeping an eye on you two. Someone's got to!'

The pottery was an outbuilding, once a stable. The floor was flagged and splashed with mud; a kiln filled one corner and on shelves all around the walls were pots and vases and bowls, propped, stacked, piled in boxes.

As they walked in their shoes crunched clay; the clammy smell of it rose about them. Huw touched the wheel by the window; it spun round, heavily, its sides ridged with dried splashes.

'What sort of thing do you want?' Hal sat on a stool, watching them. 'Take your pick.'

There were vases and jugs and plant-pots, all of them glazed with strange iridescent colours; sea-greens, blues, splashes of gold that seemed to shimmer in the shade. Their shapes were smooth and high, opening gracefully at the top; others were gnarled and twisted, like pieces of tree-trunk tangled with leaves and creepers. These were earth-coloured, dusky greens. Lizzie picked one up, turning it in her hand. 'The colours are wonderful.'

'I'm glad you think so.'

'But aren't they expensive?'

He smiled wryly. 'Just now you thought they might be cheap.'

'Where do you get the clay from?' Huw asked.

'Buy it in.' Hal flipped open the lid of the clay-bin. 'Though I've been experimenting with some from the river.' He reached in and dug out a handful with his fingers, rolled it into a lump and threw it to Huw. 'It's not too bad. A bit sticky.'

It was heavy, and soft, strangely glutinous. Huw squeezed it, leaving great wet furrows in it, then he rolled it smooth between his palms, pulling and stretching it, enjoying the watery texture. It made him think of infant school, the long sunlit classroom, full of noise and stale dinner smells.

Hal and Lizzie were talking prices; Phil wandered along the shelves picking up brushes and pots of glaze. Huw rubbed the clay against his fingers. It seemed to move, as if it squirmed and twisted in his grip. For a moment he thought there was something in it, something struggling to shape itself, into an oval, into a face, and that one thin crack where the clay had folded was a mouth.

He gripped it tight, obliterating it. Then he flung it back into the bin.

Phil stared. 'What's up? It won't bite you.'

Silent, Huw wiped his hands on his sleeve. Then he went to the door, and leaned on it, breathing deep.

Lizzie finally bought a vase; purple-blue and gold, all the colours marbled and streaked. Hal wrapped it for her in some newspaper from a damp corner.

He led them back through the gardens. Long terraced walks wound down the steep hillside like wide green steps, high with seeding grasses. Rhododendron, once neatly trimmed, grew in straggly heaps; hemlock sprouted as high as Huw's head. All the stones were cracked and flaking, with bramble creeping over them, and as he brushed ivy from a stone lion its face peered out at him, rain-worn and mossed.

'Like a house in a ghost story,' he muttered to Lizzie.

She nodded. 'Beautiful though.'

'Not much good if it's falling apart.' Huw glanced at Hal, walking ahead. 'You'd think he'd do something.'

'Perhaps he likes it like this.'

'No money, more like.'

'And there's the curse.' Phil had dropped back; he whispered it, slyly.

Huw flicked a glance at him. 'Do you believe that?'

'Maybe.'

They came to more steps, which split into a tiny maze of stone stairs, balustrades, lost urns, and in the centre a sundial, leaning askew.

Lizzie went down a few steps, brushing the purple toadflax that webbed the walls. Everything ran wild; the sundial was cut off in an ocean of nettles.

She felt the others behind her, silent.

'How do you like my garden?' Hal was waiting on the steps.

'Very much. But it's too overgrown.'

He walked down slowly, hands in pockets. 'That's because I've got no time to do anything about it.' He looked round. 'It's always been like this. I don't remember it any differently. Once I suppose there were gardeners and under-gardeners. Not now. The past is being buried. Perhaps that's right.'

'I don't see why.' Phil tugged a tall stem out of the soil and nearly overbalanced. He grinned at Huw, but Huw was pale, preoccupied. He rubbed at his hands.

'We'll do it for you!' Lizzie turned suddenly, her eyes bright with the idea. Look Hal – I can call you Hal, can't I? – we've got nothing to do really . . .'

'Speak for yourself,' Phil muttered.

'. . . and we can make it look good, like it used to.'

'You?'

'Why not! You could even pay us, if you want. We'd come cheap.' She turned on the others. 'Wouldn't we?'

For a second they were too surprised to answer. Then Phil laughed. 'If there's money in it, count me in.'

Huw nodded too, slowly. Hal knew something about the fire, on the hill. It might be a chance to find out more.

Hal was watching them all. 'Don't be ridiculous, Lizzie. Your brother isn't old enough.'

'It wouldn't be a real job. We'd come when we wanted, and you could pay us what you like. It's just . . .' she glanced sidelong at Huw, 'it would be good to have something to do.'

Hal had noticed the look. Something flickered in his eyes, a pain that surprised her, and he looked down, scratching his cheek with one hand. 'In this heat you'd soon give up.'

She knew he understood. He'd seen this was for Huw.

'We wouldn't.'

'Besides, it's too late. Nothing can save this place.'

'Rubbish!' She caught his arm. 'Please say yes, Hal. Just to see what happens. It can't do any harm, can it?'

Hal shrugged, still uneasy. For a moment she thought he would refuse, and the plan would be spoiled. Then he said, 'Well I can't pay you much. But if you really want to come, Lizzie, I suppose you can.'

CHAPTER 7

There was a glossy black beetle under the hedge, rustling through the grass and dead leaves.

Huw watched it, irritably. He hadn't slept well again last night, and he was tired, and the tiny scrape of its shell against the crisp leaves got on his nerves; nothing else moved in the heat. Above him the sky was a blue dome; the earth was baked hard and waterless. Even here, lying under the trees in the tall grass, he was itchy, hot, sticky with sap.

Watching the beetle creep across the end of his shoe he let his mind drift, trying to piece things together. He'd been all right until that day when the car nearly hit him. It had all begun then. Try as he might he couldn't remember anything about it. Except Hal's face, the blood running down his cheek. Why had he denied that? And why lie about the fire on the hill, because Huw could remember that, the smoke rising, how he had looked up at it . . . He got up now on his elbow and stared over at Belin's Hill, always dark. He must go up there again. And

Hal knew something too about that woman, who had been burned up there. Somehow all these things were connected.

And then there were the dreams.

With a jerk he flipped the beetle off and it fell upside down in the grass, whining like a small agitated machine.

How could he walk in his sleep? And this feeling that was growing in him of restlessness, of something that he had to do, where did it come from? He felt confused, and the old fear came back and chilled him. Perhaps there was something wrong with him. Perhaps he should tell someone.

'Huw?'

Lizzie stood over him, waist-high in grass. 'There you are! We're going to Newport, remember. Are you ready?'

'I suppose so.'

'Well don't put yourself out! It's for your wallpaper, after all.'

He stood up wearily, brushing down the seeds from his hair. 'It's just too hot.'

'Make an effort, Huw. They're doing this for you. And at least the shops are air-conditioned.'

'Liz . . .'

'And it's not just you, you know. It's not easy for any of us! Dad was Uncle Tom's brother, have you forgotten that?'

He stared at her, astonished. Lizzie never got angry.

'Oh, don't gape!' She pushed her hair from her face. 'Just . . . try a bit.'

Stricken suddenly by the look on his face, she put an arm round him.

'I do try, Liz.' For a moment he was ready to tell her, about the sleepwalk, the blurred man on the hill. Instead he turned towards the house.

'Wait a minute.' She crouched and put her hand into the grass.

A weak, persistent whine in his head suddenly faltered, and stopped.

'What was that?' he asked.

'A beetle. On its back, poor thing.'

The bus to town was stuffy, unbearably hot, and crowded with warm clumsy people jostling awkwardly against him, smelling of sweat and scent. Hay-smells and wasps drifted through the open windows. By the time he climbed out in Newport he felt sick; his shirt stuck to him and a point of pain had begun to throb behind his right temple.

The town was noisy; cars hurtled by at speed and crowds of people in brilliant summer clothes thronged the shops. Windows glinted in the sun, shining with goods and electric flickering lights, which he stood and stared at for ages before Lizzie came back and tugged him away.

She sounded annoyed, but he realised slowly, without any fear, that he hadn't heard a word she'd said.

Inside him, deep inside, the quiet mysteries of the valley nagged, were buried. And there was something he had to do, and it worried him, because he didn't know what it was. He grew strangely withdrawn; the day went past like a dream, like something happening to someone else. Lizzie talking, Phil eating ice-cream, Mrs Griffiths unfolding roll after roll of wallpaper, his own voice, far away, saying 'Yes' and 'No'. He walked in a whirlwind of sounds and sights, and none of them touched him, or was real.

Except one. Somewhere in the maze of shops, it stood out, as if there was nothing else in the world. A small book on a high shelf. The cover was a deep, twilight blue, a sky edged with trees, and the colour was the colour of his secret, deep, rich and dark; it sent a thrill through him so that he shuddered with delight. And on the blue was a face, a mask of stone with narrow eyes, waiting for him.

He didn't read the title, or even turn the pages. He just took it down and stared at it, and some time later, out in the street, found it was still in his hand. He couldn't even remember if he had paid for it.

All afternoon, through the steamy heat of the town, he walked between a nightmare and a dream. Sometimes he knew something was wrong, but the worry of the thing he had to do nagged at him, so that it was with a shock of surprise that he found himself on the bus staring at his own reflection, and then later recognised the lane, and Phil opening the farm gate, and the cows in the milkshed mooing.

At tea, briefly, he felt more normal; he looked up to find his uncle looking at him quizzically.

'I've been talking to you for ten minutes. Are you all right?'

'Headache,' he muttered, stupidly.

'He's been like that all day,' his aunt's voice said from the other room. 'Walking round like a zombie.'

Lizzie giggled, but Huw felt a surge of panic. 'Listen,' he said, hurriedly. 'I can't remember things . . . I think I'm slipping, Lizzie . . .'

'Slipping? Into what?'

But the moment was gone, and whatever he said in reply was blurred and lost, and it was hours later and he was in bed, the book in his hands.

Perhaps he read it. Afterwards he thought he had, turning the pages deep into the night, in his cluttered bedroom with one candle lit. Flames and dances, theories of strange gods, moved in his mind; he didn't understand what he read but he couldn't stop, and it confused him, it came out of the book and filled his room with a crackle of smoke, and the leaves rustled in the orchard, as if someone waited out there.

And then, as he had known he would, he found himself going downstairs. Deep inside, he knew this had happened before, but that terror was so deep it barely stirred.

'Wait for me,' he said firmly. 'I'm coming now.'

With a word to the dog he was out of the yard, running down the lanes, recklessly round bends and corners. Nothing would stop him now. His headaches were gone;

he felt clear, wild, full of energy. 'I'm coming! He yelled to the trees, to the hedges. 'Wait for me!'

Heart pounding, he raced through the empty streets of Caerleon, over the common, its grass dry as dust, past the chemist's window that cast its light on the dark street. Running feet echoed around him in doorways and alleys, as if all the ghosts of the village ran with him. Breathless he passed the church, where sticky sap from the lime trees lay like golden powder on the black pavement. Without thinking, he tugged his shoes off and walked on it slowly, delighting in the sticky flowers under his heels and between his toes, the honey smell of the hot night.

Rounding into Cross Street he stopped dead.

The excavation was deserted. Under the lampposts the pit looked deep and black and bottomless, the soil heaped around it in ominous hunched outlines. Red lights flashed, reflected in windows.

He waited, a shadow among the silent houses. This was the place. It had started here. It was waiting for him here.

He stepped to the edge of the trench and looked down, but it was black, a shadowy mouth, an entry to the under-world. And suddenly pain flashed in his head, so suddenly that his foot slipped, broke the loose edge of the earth and he fell forward, slipping down in a flurry of soil onto his knees. Eyes tight shut, he let the throb in his head ease, but it wouldn't, and it made him drive his fingers deep into the soil. He dug, fiercely, scraping up pebbles and stones and pieces of pot, flinging away the debris, blunting his hands on the black, crumbling soil. The world smelt of soil, soil and blood, filthying his face, blackening his fingers as he flung it out, driving his nails deep, scratching, scrabbling, sometimes laughing, sometimes with tears running down his face, because the wheels of the train were spinning, and his mother's cardigan was torn and soaked with damp, and the screech of the brakes was endless down the night's tunnel.

And then he touched something hard.

It moved.

Huw was suddenly still. In the mess of soil under his hands, something was stirring, rising up. Lumps of soil shifted, rolled aside. In the dimness he glimpsed something pale, and stretched out his fingers reluctantly and touched it, and it was hard and cold. He heaved it up, tugged it out, feeling the soil squirm and quiver as the stone face came up, uncovered itself, earth falling from its narrow eyes, the thin gash of its lips mocking him.

He held it in both hands.

A low whisper of wind stirred in its dark mouth.

CHAPTER 8

Phil came back from the Post Office the next morning in a state of high excitement, dumping a half sack of potatoes noisily inside the door.

'You'll never guess what's happened!'

'Somebody blew up the village,' Lizzie muttered, wiping a cup.

'Not far off.'

She stared at him. 'What?'

'Well, not the village. But someone wrecked that dig in Cross Street. Last night.' He poured some orange juice into a glass. 'You should see it! All the fences are smashed; there are pieces of glass from those red lamps scattered right down the street. The sides of the ditch are trampled in, all the markers and things are everywhere. It's just mud and mess.' He turned on a tap. 'There's a gaping hole in the bottom. That woman in overalls is furious.'

'Everyone's there, I suppose?' his mother asked.

'They're drinking outside at The Bull.'

'Have they called the police?'

'Yes, but it's a bit late.'

She laughed. 'The vicar's there.'

'Of course.' He grinned at her over the glass.

Lizzie tossed the washed knives thoughtfully into a drawer. After a while she said, 'Who would have done it? Vandals?'

'Or others,' Mrs Griffiths said darkly.

'Who?'

'Oh, no names, Lizzie. When you've lived here longer you'll know. Some don't like the excavations.'

Lizzie knew now; at least, she knew who her aunt was thinking of. Folding the tea-towel she frowned at Phil. He shrugged, unhappily. They were both thinking of what Hal had said in the street.

'He wouldn't though, would he?' she muttered to him quietly.

'I don't know. Strange family. Unstable.'

'Not like that.' She stared. 'That would be like . . .'

'Go on,' he said. 'Say it. It would be mad.'

They were silent a moment; Phil washing his glass, letting the cool water run over his hands. Then he said, 'No. Take my word for it, it was vandals. A crowd of yobs out of a pub.' He noticed Huw sitting in the orchard outside the window, and called, 'Don't you think so?'

Huw looked up from his book; his eyes hidden behind dark glasses. He nodded bleakly.

Phil laughed, and turned away. 'He hasn't heard a word I've said.'

But Huw had heard everything. He had listened in a sort of horror, his shaded eyes followed a ladybird down the margin, not even seeing it. Memories of the night before flickered through him; that terrible restlessness, the heat, the squirm of the earth in the pit.

And the thing upstairs.

He snapped the book shut, tossed it onto the grass and went in through the front, to avoid everyone. Upstairs, he locked his bedroom door and put his back against it.

The room was warm, and untidy. Rolls of wallpaper were heaped in a corner; a wasp whined in the gauze curtain.

He crossed to the bed and knelt on it. Between the bedhead and the wall, squeezed into a corner, was a small cupboard, painted green. The door was beside his pillow. He kept books in there, and his watch and a few biscuits. At the very back, in a leather wallet, were some photographs of his parents, mostly taken on holidays – his mother and father and Lizzie on a beach waving; he and Dad building a huge sand-car, wearing silly hats. One was older; his mother looking slim and shy in a pale pink dress, holding a baby. He didn't look at them often, but they were there, close to his pillow, close to his breathing. Once or twice, after the dream of the tunnel had woken him with shuddering breaths, he had pulled them out and just held them in the dark, feeling the sharp edges, the slightly sticky gloss.

Now there was something else.

He opened the cupboard carefully, almost warily. At the back something lay on the books. He put his hand in and lifted it out; soil fell from it, tiny lumps of red mud on the pale blue quilt.

Silent with fear, he turned it and held it up.

The stone head leered at him.

Its features were hacked out – dark, empty eyes, a thin, crude mouth – the mockery of a face, pitted and seamed, staring at him after two thousand years in the earth.

He couldn't look at it for long; it terrified him.

Hands shaking, he pulled an old magazine to pieces and wrapped the head hastily in it, hiding the evil glare, the thing's cold scorn. He shoved it back into the cupboard and sat back and stared at the closed door. Why had he done it? Was he going mad? He had thought the thing had moved under his fingers but that was nonsense and he shook his head impatiently. Now everyone knew, and the police would be called, and they would find out it was him.

He gripped his hands together, fiercely. No. He was safe. No one had seen him. No one had been about. Or had they? If anyone had been there, he might not have seen them. He couldn't even remember walking home.

*

62

That afternoon they went up to Henllys to begin Lizzie's project, walking slowly in the great heat, eating ice-creams that melted before the first bend in the lane. Huw was relieved to get out, but the strange heat oppressed him. The air barely stirred; few birds sang. An eerie, sultry hush hung over the valley, making even the far-off traffic hum sound languid.

There was no one at the house, so they walked down to the small garden where the sundial was and sank, sweating, onto the hot stones.

'This is ridiculous.' Phil rubbed his hair and shifted wearily into the shade. 'The radio said it might reach 92 today.'

'So?' Lizzie scratched a bite on her leg.

'So it's too hot to work!'

Secretly she agreed with him, but she was still anxious about Huw. The vicar had been right. He had that fixed, pale stare on his face now, and she saw he was gazing up at the hill-fort, as it towered over the house. He was getting obsessed by it. Suddenly she felt they were losing him, day by day, into some nightmare, into some tunnel of his own, and before she could stop herself she had reached out and caught his shoulder, tight.

He almost jumped.

'Come on.' She stood up, and began to drag handfuls of chickweed out of the sage. 'Let's get to work.'

The work was hot, and wearying. They stayed out of the sun as much as possible, but even after an hour of uprooting little was done, and they straightened and looked about them. A few stone steps stood naked of greenery, their edges cracked and splintered. Heat bounced off them and blurred the air. Half a bed of rich red soil lay clear of weeds.

'Looks better already,' Lizzie said, defiant.

Brushing a fly away Huw stooped and gathered the pile of weeds and grasses, and lifted it, feeling the soft green leaves tickle his face, smelling the rich grassy smell.

Static crackled; a burst of voices out of the air.

Heart thudding, he stared up through the wilting stems and saw, to his horror, that a policeman stood on the top of the steps, a huge man. His cap was off; he was rubbing his forehead with the back of one hand. The pale blue of his shirt shimmered.

'Hello there,' he said, looking down. 'Is Mr Vaughn about?'

'I don't think so.' Phil was undoing all the buttons on his shirt. He looked up curiously.

'I know you.' The policeman put his cap on and sat on the top step. 'Phil Griffiths, isn't it?'

Phil nodded. 'These are my cousins.'

The man looked at them both; Huw crouched quickly and dumped the greenery into a careful pile, picking up fragments of leaves. His heart hammered; sweat prickled his back.

'What are you doing?' the policeman asked, curiously.

'Helping out.' Lizzie sat down in the shade. 'A bit of gardening, I suppose you could say.'

'In this heat? How much is he paying you?'

'Nothing. At least . . . well it's just for fun.'

'Not my idea of fun.'

'It's all right,' Phil said quickly. 'I mean, he's not making us do it. Look, he might be up at the outbuildings. He's got a workshop.'

'I'm here, Phil.'

Hal was walking towards them over the grassy terrace, rolling down his sleeves. He looked the policeman over and said sourly, 'What do you want?'

The policeman's big face hardened; he stood up, tall and bulky, patches of sweat darkening his shirt.

'P C Ashe, sir. Routine enquiries. About the business in the village last night.'

'Routine? It didn't take you long to get to me, did it?' Hal sounded bitter; he sat wearily on the balustrade and stared at the policeman with a strange, uneasy look. 'What business?'

'The vandalism.' They could see that the policeman was tight-lipped with indignation. 'As for coming here, it's my duty to question anyone I see fit.'

He spared one glance sideways. 'Any of you youngsters round the High Street last night? At about midnight?'

Off-guard, they stared at him. Phil said 'No. We were all in bed.'

'That right?'

Huw realised the policeman was asking him. He shrugged. 'I was asleep.'

Hal was watching him too, a half-hidden, intent look. The policeman swung back at him 'And you . . . sir?'

'I didn't see anything,' Hal said slowly.

'But you were there, weren't you? Last night. In Cross Street.'

'Was I?' Hal's voice was tense.

P C Ashe opened his notebook. 'Apparently. We have a witness. Says she saw you, after midnight, near the –'

'So it's a crime to walk about after dark now?' Hal stood up. He was flushed, one fist clenched at his side. 'Look, what is this vandalism? What am I supposed to have done?'

'No one's accusing you,' the policeman said. He looked as if he was enjoying himself now. 'But in view of your public comments –'

'Comments?'

'About the excavation.'

Slowly, Hal's other hand gripped. Both Huw and the policeman saw it. Ashe stood steady; he closed his book. 'The site of the excavation in Cross Street was destroyed last night, some time after midnight.' He stopped. Hal was staring at him.

'Destroyed?' His anger had gone. He looked amazed. And afraid.

Ashe almost grinned. His voice was brisk. 'Totally. Someone tore a great big hole in it. So I'll ask you again,

Mr Vaughn, seeing as you were in the area at the time, do you know anything about it?'

Hal was looking towards the house. They all watched him, the policeman with a hard stare.

Then he turned and said, 'No. Nothing. I can't help you.'

The policeman nodded, sourly. 'You'll be hearing from me again,' he said. Then he strode off, towards his car.

When the noise of the engine had faded Lizzie showed Hal the work they had done. He nodded, glancing round, but he was preoccupied, uneasy. Once he looked at Huw, a long look.

Huw kept his head down. He went back to tearing out the weeds; there was something fascinating in it, the snapping, cracking stems dribbling milky froth; rooting up all the flat, fleshy tangles of hogweed and henbane. It helped him to get calm again, not to think, about the police, about the stone head waiting for him in the cupboard.

His fingers stubbed on something cold and hard; his heart pounded, but that was stupid. Almost angrily he dragged the stems away.

A small stone seat lay under the tangle. Carved behind it in the wall were some letters, dark and angular.

'Look at this,' Huw muttered.

They crowded behind him, darkening it; when he stood aside sunlight lit the stone. 'R.V. 1608.'

'It's hers,' Lizzie said, excited, 'Rowena!' Then she remembered Hal, and glanced at him, doubtfully.

'You know the story,' Hal said quietly.

'Phil told us.'

He was silent for a moment; then he said, 'Cover that up, Huw. Please. I have enough ghosts haunting me.'

Surprised, Huw pushed the greenery back. Hal stood up.

'Come up to the workshop, and have something to drink.'

The pottery was cool; a new row of vases stood on one shelf. Hal gave them all orange juice in glazed mugs, and they drank thirstily while he moved restlessly round the workshop, rolling a small ball of clay in his fingers.

'Did you see it?' he asked at last, leaning against the bench.

'See what?'

He didn't look up. 'The excavation. The damage.'

'I did.' Phil put down the mug. 'What a disaster. Almost as if,' he grinned, wryly, 'as if something underneath pushed its way up.'

'Don't!' Lizzie said.

They both laughed; Huw managed a strained smile. Hal watched them. Then he straightened. 'Thanks for your help,' he said, and walked quickly out, towards the house.

Lizzie looked out of the door after him. 'Come on. We'll be late. Come on, Huw.'

He made no move, so she turned, irritated.

'Huw?'

He was staring at the bench. Resting on the top, leering at him with an evil, lopsided mouth, was a small lump of clay, shaped like a head, still wet and soft. Its shadowy eyes squinted up at him.

He recognised it at once.

It was a perfect copy.

CHAPTER 9

Huw unrolled the wallpaper and held it up. 'Do you like it?' his uncle said doubtfully, leaning an arm on the sloping ceiling.

'Yes.'

'You don't sound too sure.'

'I'd forgotten what I'd picked.' In fact he stared at the blue paper blankly, knowing he'd never seen it before. What was happening to him? Was he walking round in a dream?

Perhaps his uncle noticed. 'Well, if you're sure, I'll put it up on the weekend.' He pulled himself upright and looked round the room awkwardly. 'Paint the place too – it needs it. Those cupboards.'

He moved across the room; Huw froze in alarm, but his uncle didn't go near the cupboard. Instead he pulled out a measuring tape and stretched it out on the wall where the shelves would be. His shoulders flexed under the pale shirt. From the back, Huw thought, rolling the paper, it could be Dad.

Moths fluttered against the bulb in the ceiling. The evening air smelt of silage and lavender.

'Have you . . . how are you finding it here?' Uncle Tom asked quietly.

'OK. Fine, thanks.'

'Good. It's just that,' he folded the tape with a snap and fiddled with it, his back to Huw, 'sometimes you seem a bit . . . well, as if you're not getting on so well. Not happy.' Then he grimaced. 'Sorry. Stupid word. At the moment none of us are happy.'

Huw felt his face turning red. Tears pricked suddenly behind his eyes; he felt hot and stubborn.

'I'm OK,' he muttered.

'Well, that's fine.' Still not looking round, Uncle Tom opened the door. 'Fancy a cup of tea?'

'In a minute.' When his uncle had gone he cleared his clothes off the chair and pulled it to the window, kneeling on it, with his elbows on the sill. Belin's Hill was a black mass under the faint stars.

Why didn't they leave him alone? Always prodding, always asking questions. If he was all right. How did he know? If he was seeing things; no, but maybe that was normal, maybe it was. He should ask, but he didn't want to ask. He didn't want anyone to know.

The cupboard was behind him; he didn't look at it, but he was aware of the thing that was in it, as if even through the wooden door it glared at his back. He should get rid of it, dump it out there in the woods or the river, before someone found it. Found out. But he hated the thought of touching it. He knew what it was. Long ago the Celtic people had made heads like that – stone faces, of gods, demons, heroes. They had collected real ones, too, the heads of enemies. They fed them, with blood, people's lives.

And Hal knew. He must know. Huw thought again about the clay lump on the pottery bench; how the soft mud had squirmed under his fingers as he'd picked it up, twisting the face into grotesque wrinkles.

'What is it?' Lizzie had said, but he'd closed his fist on it before she could see, obliterating the leering mouth with the great furrowmarks of his fingers. Then he had rolled it smooth and thrown it away, into the weed-choked yard.

Only Hal could have made it. It explained things. Hal must have seen him, last night at the dig, seen what he did and what he'd taken. That was why he'd lied to Ashe. And now he'd left this as a warning. To say he wouldn't take the blame for something he hadn't done.

Miserably, Huw rubbed his face. He should go to the police and own up, but how could he? He thought of his uncle in a police station; the bewilderment on his face.

The room was dim. Downstairs his uncle filled the kettle, water thrumming against tin.

Then, in the room, something moved.

He lifted his head, listening.

Silence seemed to breathe near him, at his shoulder, on his cheek.

It came again, a soft scrape of sound.

Quickly, he turned.

Nothing had changed. Books and boxes lay stacked on the floor; a pile of clothes littered the bed.

And then across the dark room he heard a soft, muffled thud.

It came from inside the cupboard.

His skin crawled; he caught his breath and was instantly at the light switch, snapping it on. Brightness filled the warm air; he was staring in horror at the cupboard's closed door when another sound erupted outside, a long, eerie moan and whimper that made his heart pound until he recognised it.

The dog was howling!

He ran to the window. The orchard was shadowy, full of flitting movement, light dappling the leaves. His own shadow stretched crazily over the grass, and beyond, on Belin's Hill, he saw lights. Small, red flickers, like torches.

'REX!'

Huw jumped. The kitchen door had opened below; his uncle came out in a great rectangle of yellow light.

'What's the matter with you! Stop that row!'

The dog yelped and was silent; his dark shape rattling the chain. Uncle Tom bent over him. 'All right. What's the matter, eh?'

He turned and looked up, and in the window Huw's sight blurred; pain throbbed in his head. He saw a stranger looking up at him, a face smeared with greens and browns, painted marks, winding tattoos.

'Huw,' it said quietly.

'What?' he breathed. 'What do you want!'

'Did you see what it was? That frightened the dog?'

He shut his eyes, gripping the windowframe tight, and shook his head. He heard the dog's paws pad on the tiles, and then the door slammed.

When he looked out again the night was silent; the hill was dark.

He turned, ran to the cupboard, tugged it open and dragged out the head. As he carried it across the room the paper dislodged; half of the face leered up at him; one dark narrow eye. With a hiss of fear Huw wrapped it up again hastily, flung it into the bottom of his wardrobe and jammed the slippery key in the lock, his hands sweating as he forced it round.

It must have slipped, he thought, over and over. Must have toppled. Not moved.

Downstairs was quiet and normal, the dog asleep by the window. The television spoke to itself in a corner until Uncle Tom switched it off, irritated. 'Now who's this?'

Headlights swept into the yard, the crunch of car wheels. After a moment his wife came in, Phil and Lizzie and the vicar all talking behind her.

'Had a lift,' she said brightly.

They sat at the table and drank tea, and Huw sat on the

broad windowseat, looking out into the still night, listening, uneasy.

'You'd think it would be cooler in the evenings,' his aunt complained, pushing her hair back. 'The nights are too hot to sleep. Gives you bad dreams, this weather.'

'And the strange thing is, it's only here.' The vicar sipped from his mug. '"Local pressure conditions in the Usk Valley," according to the radio. It's most bizarre.'

'It's putting the cows off,' Tom Griffiths muttered. Then he said, 'What's your view on this vandalism business?'

Huw almost groaned. Then, for a moment he thought he heard a sound upstairs; he glanced up, nervously.

Mitchel noticed. 'You look tired, Huw. Any more headaches?'

'Now and then.'

The vicar nodded. Then he said, 'I don't know what to think about it, Tom.'

'The police were up at Henllys,' Phil put in, quietly.

'Oh surely they don't suspect Hal?' Mitchel frowned. 'That's ridiculous.' He took out a cigarette.

'Hal Vaughn.' Uncle Tom shook his head, considering. 'Strange lad. Remember when they wanted to dig on Belin's? Turned them down flat. Temper like his dad's. Not that I mean . . .'

'The villagers shut him out,' the vicar said, flicking his lighter off, 'so it's hardly surprising.' He leaned back and blew out smoke contentedly. Then he saw Phil's grin.

'Feel free to smoke,' Mrs Griffiths said icily.

'Oh I'm so sorry! I do keep forgetting! Do you mind if I . . .?'

She smiled at him. 'No. I suppose not.'

'Bad for me, I know. You don't have to say.'

'And everyone round you,' Lizzie muttered.

After three cigarettes and as many cups of tea the vicar left, walking out through the dark orchard to his car. To his surprise, Huw wandered out with him.

'Everything all right?' Mitchel asked.

'Yes, thanks.'

'Good.' The vicar breathed the warm night air contentedly. 'If you ever need anyone to talk to, Huw . . .'

'It's not that.' Huw put his hand on the car, feeling the warm metal. Then he looked up. 'Will Hal really get the blame?'

'Good Lord no. The whole idea is nonsense.' Mitchel put the key in the car door and turned it thoughtfully. 'I know Hal, perhaps better than anyone else. To act like that would be beneath his pride.' Then he said, 'May I ask why you're concerned?'

'I know he didn't do it. I just thought . . . well, people talk.'

The vicar nodded, opening the door. 'You remind me of Hal in some ways.' He paused again, and said, 'Do you know anything about the excavation, Huw?'

Huw stared at him. 'No,' he whispered.

For a moment they looked at each other, the vicar's eyes

shrewd and sharp. Then he slid into the car and rolled the window down.

'Goodnight, Huw,' he said.

Half an hour later Huw went up to bed. He switched on the light in his room and stood stockstill in the doorway.

From his pillow the stone head leered at him.

CHAPTER 10

Each day seemed hotter.

Sun blazed on the green valley, scorching the grass, baking roads and pavements until the air steamed and quivered, a cauldron of heat. Standpipes went up in the streets, fires were banned on the tinder-dry hillsides. Every farmer from Caerleon to Usk stared moodily at their shrunken, withered pastures.

In the village, the doors were propped permanently open, and faded awnings drooped over the windows of the shops like half-closed eyelids. Wasps were everywhere, and flies, and no one walked in the white-heat of the sun, but kept to the shade, crossing and re-crossing the narrow, winding streets.

From the pub window the vicar watched Hal pass and lean his hands on the red and white fence, looking down into the ruined excavation. He stayed there a long time, staring, attentive, as if he could see into the churned soil and muddy hollow at the heart of the pit. A few passers-by watched him curiously.

The vicar swallowed a small ice-cube from his glass and sucked it, feeling the cold burn his mouth. He liked Hal – liked him a lot – but he was touchy and quick to take offence. This wasn't going to be easy.

When Hal walked into The Bull a moment later, he looked around, almost warily.

The vicar raised his glass. 'Over here.'

A few heads turned; the darts match in the corner paused.

Ignoring them, Hal said quietly, 'Can I get you anything?'

Mitchel drained his glass. 'Another of these, please. Nice cold orange.'

Hal crossed to the bar. He looked strained and tense. 'Orange. Half of bitter. And some water for the dog.'

Des Phillips, the landlord, put down his polishing cloth and drew the beer slowly. 'I saw you looking at the excavation out there.' He put the glass down and added, 'Nasty mess someone made.'

Hal gave him a dark glance. The man's eyes were shrewd and alert. 'So they did.' He slid some money across, carried the drinks carefully, then went back for the dog's water, in an old battered dish.

They're all watching him, the vicar thought, with sudden foreboding. He caught the eye of a few of the darts players; they turned away or nodded, awkwardly. The game started up again.

Hal gave the dish to the dog, who lapped at it thirstily,

splashing the dusty wooden floor with tiny silver bubbles of water. The room was hazy with sun, the doors and windows open.

'So why here?' Hal said quietly. 'Is this is a show of faith?'

Mitchel put his feet up on a chair and blew out smoke. He was smiling. 'If you mean do I believe these ridiculous rumours about the dig, of course I don't.'

'You must be the only one.' Hal glanced round, sourly; ten pairs of eyes flicked away.

The vicar nodded, serious now. 'I heard the police had been round. It's a disgrace. Tell me, Hal, does it bother you?'

For a while Hal didn't answer. Then he said, 'They all think the same thing: His father. Now him.'

An edge of pain was raw in his voice; the vicar did not miss it. A wasp floated over the orange juice; he waved it away.

'You don't usually talk about your father.'

The dog whimpered under the table; Hal nudged it with his foot. 'Nothing to say,' he said, harshly. 'Look, John, why do you want to see me? Not just to show them I've still got one friend?'

The vicar grinned. 'Not just that.' He ground the cigarette end slowly into the stained ashtray. 'Fact is, Hal, I've got a favour to ask. It's a bit of an imposition, I know . . .'

'What?'

The vicar seemed reluctant. He folded his yellow-stained

fingers together. 'You remember I asked you to lend me the house?'

'I said no.'

'I know you did. And I'd booked the village hall for the concert. Tomorrow night. But it's too small, Hal. I've sold over two hundred seats, and I went round there today to look at it. They'll never all fit in! Half of them will be sitting on the pavement.'

Hal smiled briefly, unhappily. 'I'm sorry. But I don't see –'

'That's just it. You can help. I need a bigger hall. I'm in a mess.'

'You want Henllys.'

'Er . . . yes.' Despite himself the vicar felt guilty. Hal looked bitter and strained; this business with the dig seemed to be upsetting him. Or perhaps he thought Mitchel's friendship came at a price. The vicar hurried on. 'I wouldn't press you, but I'm desperate, Hal. I'll hire the hall of course, pay you a reasonable sum . . .'

'It's out of the question.'

'Please Hal, let me –'

'NO!'

The sudden insistence of the word made the barkeeper turn, curious. Conversation sank to an interested hush.

Mitchel played with his lighter. He knew he had asked a lot, had been clumsy, and he felt annoyed with himself. Hal stared darkly out of the window, moodily picking bits of clay from his fingers. When he spoke again his voice was quiet.

'I couldn't.'

'Ah well. I suppose I understand.'

'You don't, John.' He wiped moisture from the outside of his glass, leaving a pale clay-coloured streak. 'That house is full of echoes. And it's dying; going back to the soil, being overgrown. That's the way it should be. The house and the family and the curse.'

Uneasy, the vicar straightened and took his feet off the chair. 'You shouldn't be thinking like that. You can't blame your family history on a curse.'

'You know I can!' Hal glanced up at him suddenly. 'You know what happened to us! She haunts us, haunts the house. All of us, one by one, generation by generation. In the end my father never slept, do you know that? He'd prowl the house all night, hiding from her, sobbing in fear of her, and I'd lie awake listening to him, and there was nothing I could do. Nothing!' His fingers were trembling; he clenched them tight.

In the silence traffic hummed in the street. The heat seemed even more intense. Mitchel wiped his neck with a damp handkerchief. The talk of ghosts disturbed him.

'I'm sorry, Hal. I shouldn't have asked.' He put the handkerchief away and thoughtfully traced a pattern in the split beer. 'But let me say this. I know the house means a lot to you. But I don't think you should let . . . Rowena defeat you. If a curse can be put on, it can be ended. You can start again.'

Hal smiled and shook his head ruefully. 'You sound like Lizzie.'

'Lizzie?'

'Griffiths. She wants to restore the grounds.'

'And why not!' Mitchel leaned forward. 'Why not bring light and music and voices back to the house, Hal, just for one night? Defy all the ghosts. Can I ask you, please, to consider it. For my sake.'

Hal was silent, rolling a clay ball between his fingers. The vicar sensed his wavering mood. 'It's for a good cause. The church needs repairs. Especially the chapels.' He lit another cigarette, deciding not to mention the Vaughn tombs. 'We'd only use the hall, and a room for teas. I'd have everything cleared up afterwards. Absolutely no one would go into any other part of the house. And forgive me, Hal, but I know you need the money.'

Hal shrugged. 'Everyone knows that.'

Mitchel looked out at the excavation, nodding. Hot air rippled over the torn pit.

'How long?' Hal asked it with an effort.

'We'd come at six. Finished and out by eleven.' He tapped the cigarette on the ashtray.

'All right.' Hal pushed the empty glass away wearily. 'All right, but no one, John, anywhere else in the house.'

'Of course!' The vicar was delighted. 'I'm so relieved! It's such a weight off my mind.' He chuckled. 'Lots of people will be curious to see the place – it might even add to the numbers.'

Hal glanced up sharply. 'It's not a tourist attraction. I don't want to see anyone. Don't forget.'

'Not at all. I promise you.' Mitchel smiled, relieved, thinking it was time to change the subject. 'Well, I'm glad that's settled. So. I wonder what really went on out there the other night?'

It was a bad choice; Hal stood up, abruptly. The dog lifted its head. 'Nothing good, be sure of that.' He turned quickly and walked to the door. 'Tomorrow, at six. I'll leave the door open.'

'Thanks again.'

The vicar watched him fade into the shimmer of the street, then drank the last of the orange juice, feeling a little guilty. Was he really becoming something of a bully? And if he hadn't known better he would have suspected Hal knew something about the wrecked dig. Then he thought of Huw Griffiths last night. The boy was deeply disturbed. Not surprising, after his parents' death. A tragedy like that might easily lead to erratic behaviour. Perhaps it already had.

Far along the hushed street the clock chimed ten. He got up, lazily, and took the glass to the bar.

'Thanks, Des. I wonder –'

A crash interrupted him, and a scream, half-stifled. A dart player threw and missed and swore.

The barmaid had gone to clean the table; she stood there quite still for a second, then bent down and began to pick up the pieces of Hal's glass, bit by bit, from the floor.

The vicar went back.

'Something scare you? Wasps?'

'Her?' Des Phillips laughed. 'Take a bit to do that!'

'But it did, Des. It gave me a start.' As she looked up, Mitchel saw her face was drawn and white.

'What did?'

'That. That thing.'

He went closer and picked it up from the ashtray. A round knob of hardening clay moulded into the image of a head, the eyes narrow, without pupils, the mouth a thin, lipless gash. It leered up at him, unpleasantly.

Reluctant, he carried it to the bar.

'What the hell is that?' Phillips stared in disgust.

'Not yours then?'

'Never seen it before. Evil-looking thing.'

'Perhaps someone left it there,' the vicar muttered.

'There's only been you and Vaughn over there, though the window's always open. Didn't you see it, when you were sitting there?'

Mitchel stared down at it, without answering.

CHAPTER 11

Sweating under a single thin sheet, Huw lay in bed, staring at the head. It leered at him through the closed glass of the window, the sunlight twisting the gash of its mouth to a smirk.

He had thrust it out there last night in despair, not knowing what else to do with it; slamming the window down, he had scrambled into bed with his face to the wall. But all night he had felt its stare, through the glass, through the sheet, through his shoulderblades, so that he'd tossed and turned on the burning pillow, drifting between the nightmares of the train and the bubbling earth, and that hard, mocking stare.

Once he had woken with a jerk, drenched in sweat. Rigid, in an agony of listening, he knew it had moved.

It had thumped against the window.

For a long time, hours maybe, he had stared at the dim flowers on the wall, afraid to turn his head, afraid to sleep, until sometime in the early morning the flowers had drifted into bricks, the bricks of the tunnel, the fronds of the ferns damp against his cheek.

Now it was light, and he was tired. But he knew he had to do something. Today.

He dressed quickly, tugging on an old T-shirt and trousers. He found a plastic bag, tipped the model cars out of it and crossed to the window. Taking a deep breath, he looked at the head.

It looked back, cold and subtly amused.

What are you? He thought. Where do you come from? What do you want from me!

The head stared. Huw steadied himself, told himself to shut up. He fought down the fear, the thudding of his heart. The thing couldn't answer him; it wasn't alive.

He opened the window slowly, and picked up the head. It felt cold, damp with dew. A tiny droplet glinted in the eye socket.

He stared at it, then plunged it deep into the bag, tied knot after knot over it, ran downstairs and flung it into the dustbin, slamming the lid down.

He stood back.

The rubbish was collected today. He would be rid of it then.

It was at dinnertime, stirring his untasted salad about in astonishment, that he heard about the others. Unpacking her groceries, his aunt talked quickly and absently. There had been one in the pub and one in the Post Office and one perched on a ledge by the church door. The vicar had collected them all. 'He's shown them to those people at the dig,' Aunt Ffion said, tugging out a bag of sugar.

'What are they?' Huw's voice was sharp with anxiety; he bent his head and cut up a tomato, as if he wasn't bothered.

'Some sort of copies of some Celtic thing. God knows. Now, this afternoon Tom's starting on your room, Huw. It'll be half-finished by the time you come back.' She glanced down at him, then sat in the empty chair. Her voice softened. 'We'll really have it looking good. Then you can arrange all your books and things. Make it just like home.'

Phil gave his mother a warning look; but she was watching Huw.

'Is the salad all right?'

'Yes. I'm not really hungry though. It's too hot.'

As he drank orange juice he watched her turn back to the shopping, and felt wretched. They were only trying to be kind, but how could he care about wallpaper with this hanging over him. What was Hal doing? Why was he making all these things? He looked at Lizzie, reading the paper. For a moment he wanted to get her alone, pour out everything, but it would mean telling her about the dig, what he'd done. He couldn't. They'd have him back in that hospital, for one thing. And now these things were everywhere, mocking him, tormenting him. He rubbed his forehead wearily. The only thing to do was speak to Hal. He hated the idea.

The vicar had asked them to help with the concert in return for free tickets, though all Lizzie wanted was to look inside Henllys. They walked up that afternoon; the gardens were deserted as usual, shimmering in a green heat of wasps and weeds, and though Huw made an excuse to go round to the pottery, the workshop was empty.

He opened the door and stood there a moment looking round, at the kiln, the terracotta pots, the vases. Hal was a craftsman. He was very clever at his work.

In the late afternoon the vicar drove up in a borrowed van full of chairs, and they helped him carry them into the long hall flagged with uneven tiles. It was cool, and smelt musty. At one end a great fireplace opened in the dark panelling; strange foliage was carved around it, with tiny faces peering from the smooth brown leaves. Huw glanced away, frowning. The hall windows were casements, leaded with glass diamonds. Opening one, Lizzie knelt on the windowseat and looked down the overgrown terraces to the cauldron of the valley.

A faint breeze swished the grasses. There was no other sound.

'It's so quiet here!'

Huw nodded. Far below, he could see the green refuse lorry crawling through the lanes. He thought of the black plastic sacks piled at the farm gate. At least he would be rid of one problem.

'Come on, come on,' the vicar said, rolling his sleeves up. 'Let's get on!'

Phil dropped a pile of chairs with a groan. 'Whose idea was this!'

'Mine,' Lizzie said. 'And it'll get the fat off you.'

They worked hard for an hour and a half, getting the chairs in, arranging them, setting up tables for teas, putting out programmes. Once Huw found the vicar on his own, groping under the van's dashboard for cigarettes. 'Never take up this habit, Huw,' he said, lighting one and sighing.

'I won't,' Huw said absently. He drummed his fingers on the hot metal. 'My aunt was saying you'd found some things. Around the village. Heads.'

Mitchel nodded, looking at him through the blue smoke. 'Celtic ritual heads. Or rather, crude modern copies. All around the place.' He leaned forward suddenly. 'Do you know what I think, Huw? I think whoever wrecked the dig is making them. Now why should that be, I wonder?'

Confused, Huw stared back. 'I don't know,' he stammered.

The vicar watched him, then pushed the floppy fair hair from his forehead. 'No,' he murmured quietly. 'Perhaps you don't.'

There was no sign of Hal all day, as if he was deliberately keeping away, and at about seven o'clock the first cars began to arrive, purring up the rutted track. The sounds of engines and banging doors and laughter began to disturb the peace, sounding strange here and alien, as if, as Lizzie said, something asleep a long time was being woken.

The house looked different too, its downstairs windows brightly lit and glowing over the valley. People began to come in, quietly at first, then noisier, meeting friends. They found their seats and looked around curiously at the panelled hall, the closed doors that led out of it, the ornate fireplace. Moths fluttered and danced in the open windows.

Outside, the sun sank, a red ball, into the steam and mists of the hot evening. Lizzie went and sat at the door with Phil, collecting tickets where it was cool, and the small orchestra tuned up with strange squeals and ripples of sound. It was half past seven. The audience hushed; the vicar began his 'few words'.

'Where's Huw?' Lizzie whispered.

Phil shrugged, counting pound coins. 'Haven't seen him for a while.'

The music started, swelling in the dark room. She looked at the dim heads of the audience, but there was no sign of him.

'Do you think he's all right?'

'Outside, I expect. Don't worry, he'll be in.'

In fact Huw was just outside in the porch, listening nervously. In the moment before the music had started he had heard something else, a murmur of sound that puzzled him.

It had come from far off in the house, behind a small wooden door down some steps.

He looked at it, considering. John Mitchel had warned

them not to wander off. But it might be Hal, and he needed to talk to Hal.

He opened the door, quietly.

Behind it was a long corridor, ending in shadows. The floor was flagged with stone slabs, and there were a few dark doorways on each side. Carefully, he slipped in, closing the door behind him with a soft click.

He listened. There was nothing now but the music; a violin and cello playing something mournful and rather eerie. He walked forward slowly, the creak of his shoes loud in the hush. The house was empty, and dark. It was cooler than outside, almost chill, as if the walls were thick. Music rose and fell behind him. He stopped, one hand on the wall.

'Hal?'

His voice was small and doubtful. Nothing moved in the shadows: then something dripped on his hand, an ice-cold splash that made him jerk with fear. Heart thudding, he looked up.

A grey stain of damp spread down the wall.

At its far end the passage turned suddenly into a dark hallway; there was a narrow staircase climbing up into shadows. He guessed he was near the kitchens, that this would have been the servants' stairs, when the house had had servants. Carefully, barely breathing, he crossed to its foot and looked up, one hand on the smooth wooden ball of the banister.

The sound was there, faint, familiar behind the swell of violins.

A choking sound.

Uneasy, Huw began to climb, his hand sliding up the rail. The staircase creaked, turned ahead of him. It was bare of carpet. One tiny square window pierced the deep wall, so masked outside by ivy that its light was a strange green gloom. Through clustering leaves he saw gates, the corner of a yard.

Far behind, a splatter of applause burst out in the hall, making his heart lurch. The landing was dark and dusty. Blackness hung around him like a curtain. And yet, in front of him was a narrow slit of light, down at floor level. It was a dim, warm red light, flickering.

Like firelight, under a door.

As he crept nearer it lit his hands and face, and he saw it ripple on his outstretched fingers. Inside the room, someone was laughing.

Very softly, subtly amused.

And there was a crackle and spit of flames; a creak of movement, like a chair.

He waited, fingers on the curved handle. He knew it wasn't Hal. It was a woman. His heart was thudding like a hammer; pain nagged behind his forehead. Slowly, very slowly, he pushed the handle down and let the door swing silently inwards.

The room was empty.

For a long moment he stood by the door; then he came in and closed it, watching the long shafts of red light slanting in through the uncurtained windows. They fell across the floor in great rectangles, onto the cold grey ashes of the fireplace.

She had gone.

He ungripped his fists, breathed out, feeling the tension lessen. But she had been here. Just then. He had almost seen her.

It was a library, or had been. A tall old clock ticked noisily in one corner; a few books stood on the dusty shelves. Above the fireplace, in a great gilt frame, the portrait of a woman gazed down at him. There was no name, but he knew this was Rowena. Calmly she stared past him, dark-haired, narrow-eyed, her red brocade dress dimmed behind centuries of grime.

He gazed up at her. 'Tell me what's happening,' he muttered. 'Why the valley is burning up. What is there on the hill. What does it want?'

The sunset touched her; a draught stirred the ashes. He stood alone in the slanting scarlet light, his shadow long and thin.

Then he heard it; someone coming up the stairs, a quick, light step. Hide! He thought, in panic. But it was too late.

The door opened.

Hal came in and saw him.

CHAPTER 12

Huw felt hot with embarrassment.

He stood, small and foolish in the fiery light; Hal stared at him, then closed the door quietly. He said nothing.

The dog leapt up onto a windowseat and lay there, chin on paws.

The silence was terrible.

'I was looking at the picture,' Huw muttered at random.

Hal ignored that. 'Why did you come up here?'

He hardly knew what to say. 'Just . . . looking about.'

'No other reason?'

'I thought I heard someone.'

Hal leaned against the fireplace. He seemed surprisingly calm. His shirt was splashed with clay; for a moment Huw had a memory glimpse of the man on the hill, his clothes the colours of forest and earth, blurred and uncertain.

'It might be a good thing. I've been wanting to talk to you, Huw.'

Fear rose in him. He wanted to get away; not to hear this. But Hal went on, relentless.

'I know about the excavation. I know that it was you.'

Hot, his back pricking with sweat, Huw turned and stared out of the window, seeing nothing. He wanted to deny it, to say he'd been asleep in bed at Phil's, but he couldn't. He gripped his hands to stop them shaking.

Hal waited a moment, watching. Then he said, 'You needn't worry. No one else knows. And I'm not going to tell them.'

'Yet.'

'I won't.' He paused. 'Look, I think I understand some of this. If you talk to me, I could help.'

Furious, Huw spun around. 'Do you? Well, I don't understand! And you've got a peculiar way of keeping quiet!'

'What do you mean?'

'I mean these clay heads! You know what I mean!'

Hal stared at him so strangely that for the first time he felt a twinge of doubt. Sullenly Huw muttered, 'Those clay heads. In the village. It had to be you. You saw me, saw what I took out of the pit, and you –'

'Wait!' In the red light Hal looked tense. Huw saw how his hand gripped the mantelpiece. 'This is worse than I thought. Sit down. Let's get it straight.'

Reluctantly, Huw sat on the edge of the windowseat.

Hal rubbed his hair. Then he said, 'First of all, I didn't see you at the pit and I didn't know you'd taken anything out of it. It must have been a few minutes later that I saw you – you were walking up the lane towards me, on your way home. I said "Good night", or something, but you walked straight by as if I wasn't there. You hadn't heard me, hadn't even seen me, as if you were sleepwalking. And Mick was barking, and a whole pack of dogs somewhere else. The air was cold, even on that hot night; clammy, smelling of earth.' He straightened and turned, his face edged with the eerie light. 'Looking back I thought I saw something else, like a shadow. Behind you.'

He was silent, remembering. Huw watched, still as a stone.

'When the police turned up next day and you said you hadn't been there; then I realised. I know you can't explain why you did it.'

There was a pause; in it they could hear the music surge to a faint crescendo. Finally Hal said, 'What heads, Huw?'

Suddenly Huw was glad to tell him, to tell somebody. The words stammered out of him in relief.

'The thing I took – that came up from the pit – was a sort of head. A carved stone, with eyes, horrible eyes, and a thin mouth. I found it in my room next morning. I still don't remember bringing it home.' He swallowed, his mouth dry. 'Next day, up here, there was a clay one, just made. Exactly the same.'

Looking up he saw Hal watching him, eyes dark. 'There have been others. In the village. The vicar's got them.'

'And you thought –'

'I thought you'd made them. For me. A sort of message. And the real one, it scares me . . .' A sudden edge of fear touched him. 'But if you didn't make them, who did?'

Hal shook his head. 'Maybe no one. Maybe the thing replicates itself, now it's out, in the soil and the clay; in the mind, too.'

'I won't believe that!' Huw said hotly. 'It's impossible.'

'That depends on what it is.'

'Then what is it! Do you know?'

The clock ticked. His question seemed to hang like the dust. Then Hal crossed the room into the fading red glow; he crouched at Huw's side. 'Listen, Huw,' he said. 'Years ago a woman lived in this house –'

'Rowena.'

'You know about her?'

'Phil told us. But I don't see what –'

'Oh, she has everything to do with it.' Hal looked up at the picture on the wall. 'There she is. She was a strange woman. No one knew where she came from. People disliked her. Stories went about that she walked alone at night on Belin's Hill, that she consorted with spirits, that she had woken a demon that gave her knowledge and spells. They began to call her a witch.'

Huw looked at the woman's face. Dim flecks of scarlet flickered over it, filtered through the trees outside. It gave an illusion of movement; she seemed to smile through it, knowingly.

'One night she went out from here after dark. Her two sons followed her. She went up onto the hillside, by the pillar of stone.'

'How do you know?' Huw whispered.

'There's an account of her trial in the library here. It's a bit evasive about what actually happened on the hill. It seems that she stood on the hilltop under the moon and spoke to something.' He turned away from the picture, his face shadowed. Huw saw how he looked like the woman, the same narrow skull, dark hair.

'She spoke quietly. They could only hear murmurs. The "demon", as they called it, seemed to be asking her for something, something she owed, but she kept refusing. She teased and mocked it. Then the moon came from behind a cloud, and they saw it.'

'What?' Huw said, his voice strained.

Hal looked up. 'You know what. A man with the smell of earth about him, his clothes browns and greens, his face tattooed, his hair streaked with mud. A man from the past.'

After a moment he went on. 'Someone must have made a noise. Or perhaps she knew that they were watching her all along – that would have been like her. So she said something else, loud, so they could all hear. She said "I will not pay the debt. We will ask my children, and their children, because even they have turned against me." Then she walked away, straight past her sons, and home. She was tried for witchcraft, and burned on the hill. She cursed the Vaughns right to the end.'

Standing up, he went to the fireplace again, leaning his hands on it and looking down at the ashes. With one foot he nudged them; they disintegrated with a dry whisper.

'Her curse came true. One by one she haunted them, or something haunted them. Fathers, sons, daughters. None of them lived to be old, none of them dared pay her debt, whatever it is.' He said suddenly, 'John told me your parents both died in that train crash.'

Bewildered, Huw nodded.

'You were lucky.'

'Lucky?' Huw stared, outraged.

'Yes.' He didn't look round; his voice was bitter and full of pain. 'My father took years to die. She took his mind apart piece by piece. He was afraid and ashamed and she taunted him with it. Do you know how it is, Huw, when your father doesn't even know who you are?'

Silenced, Huw stroked the dog. Its hair was long and silky. It whined and nosed his fingers, then licked them.

There was nothing he could say. He was chilled with a sickly, miserable fear, and far below them the music began again, rising up.

Finally Hal turned. He seemed to be keeping himself under some tight control. 'I'm sorry. None of that concerns you. But I know what it's like.' He looked round at the picture. 'In the last few days, I think she's come back. This time for me.'

'Who left the heads?' Huw demanded. Suddenly he was angry.

He stood up, abruptly, so that the dog whined.

Hal shrugged. 'I told you. Nobody.'

'Don't talk rubbish!'

Hal glared at him. 'I'm not a liar. Maybe they are a message, but not from me!'

'That's stupid.' Flustered, Huw stared out of the window. It was dark in the valley. Music thundered below. 'I don't believe a word of this!'

'Then what happened in Cross Street?' In a flash Hal had lost his temper too. 'What made you dig up that thing, take it home? God, Huw, you know what it is! And the fires on the hill . . . Oh, I've seen them too, don't look so shocked. I suppose you don't believe that, either?'

Huw said, 'That's just me. Something wrong with me.'

'Don't be stupid!' Furious, Hal caught him by the arm and swung him round. 'What about the heat, that's burning us all up, that began that day the car almost hit you? Don't you see, that thing was down there, waiting. You were terrified, riveted with fear. So was I. Somehow we woke it, brought it back, just as she did, centuries ago. It's alive!'

Huw watched him, stiff, pulling away. 'No. You're blaming me for something that isn't happening.' His voice was so hoarse that he hardly knew it.

'I know you're afraid . . .'

'I'm not afraid!'

'Huw —'

'No! You listen to me!' Half sobbing, half furious, he

101

squirmed out of Hal's grip. 'None of this is true! They're all dead, all of them! Rowena is dead! None of them can hurt me!'

He stormed away; oddly calm, Hal watched.

'So why did you come into this room?'

Halfway to the door, Huw stopped dead.

'I'll tell you why,' Hal said, evenly. 'Because you heard her. Didn't you?'

Despite himself, he looked back. Hal stood in the darkening, empty room. 'She's dead, yes. But you heard her.'

For a moment Huw couldn't move. Then he was gone, thundering down the stairs and along the corridor, bursting through the porch into the still night air. He ran, as if he couldn't stop, as if he could outrun fear and memory and nightmare, racing down the long dark track, leaping over ruts, tearing through branches, hurtling down the steep, twisting network of lanes and hedges.

Flinging open the farm gate Huw threw himself in, hanging over the top rail, gasping for breath, coughing, letting the night steady around him, steady and settle, until he could lean his forehead on the rotting gatepost. Sweat ran down his back; his shirt stuck to him.

'Don't let him be right,' he whispered. 'Please. Don't let him be right.'

He stayed there a long time; he was almost cold when he slipped into the house and came face to face with his aunt.

'You're home early.'

'Bit of a headache,' he muttered, pushing past her up the stairs. 'Nice surprise for you up there,' she said, laughing.

He opened the door. Three walls of the room were hung with the pale blue paper. In the twilight it looked cool and strange. A trestle table and bucket stood in a corner; the room smelt damply of paste.

'Like it?' his aunt called up.

'Yes.' His eyes found the new shelves, and fixed there.

'It's not a bad colour, is it, Huw?'

He was cold, shivering with fear.

'And I put all your bits and pieces up. Quite a collection!'

He tried to answer, but couldn't.

Across the room the stone head sneered at him.

CHAPTER 13

He dared not sleep.

He didn't trust it, not even with the light on, not even where he could see it. He left it on the shelf and huddled up on the bed, the sheet around his shoulders. But after only ten minutes he couldn't stand it; he had to turn away.

That was worse.

He lay restless, sweating. The window was wide open; the night air humming with heat. Far down the valley a car purred up the lanes.

Desperate, his thoughts wandered into dismal ways; he thought of the hospital, his long days there staring up at the ceiling. They had said he would have headaches. But visions? Sleepwalking? And if it was real as Hal said; if the thing on the hill was alive, what did it want?

It wanted him.

Movement in the room; he sat up, instantly. The bedside lamp went out, without a sound.

With a yell Huw leapt up for the lightswitch, jabbed it on, kneeling in the tangle of bedclothes.

Harsh yellow light showed him the new paper, the cluttered shelves, the head. It might have moved. It seemed nearer the front; he had been sure it was right at the back, by the sticky wall.

He had gathered himself up and crept halfway across the room before fear conquered him. He stopped, silent, and jumped back into bed. He dared not touch it. He would have to wait till daylight.

But by two o'clock he knew he would go mad if he stayed in the room any longer. Grabbing the sheet he ran to the door and crept out. The head seemed to watch him pass, its shadowy eyes long and dark.

The stairs were lit by moonlight through a window; he locked the bedroom door and slipped down to the living-room, a place of dim furniture and the faint smells of the day's meals. He curled up on the sofa, pushing newspapers aside.

Tomorrow. Tomorrow he would have to get rid of it! It was driving him mad! Somewhere where no one could bring it back.

And then no one would ever know.

Except Hal. Already, he wished he hadn't told him. But it was too late for that.

For the rest of the night Huw dozed, sometimes jerking awake, but as soon as the pale sun touched the windows he dragged himself up, tired and aching, and went back upstairs.

Cautiously he opened the door, and his skin crawled.

The head lay on his bed, toppled, on the bare mattress, as if someone had picked it up and thrown it there.

For a cold minute he stared at it, then he dressed quickly, took a sack he'd brought up from the yard and came close. After a moment's thought, he pulled out a pair of woolly gloves from a drawer and put them on, not wanting even to touch the cool clammy stone.

As he lifted it, it felt heavier. Even through the wool it tingled his fingers with a charge of power; a faint crackle of fear that murmured in the room like a burst of static.

Huw bundled it up, snatched some food from the kitchen and went out of the house quickly, running through the orchard in the early morning sunlight. Everyone else was asleep.

He had no plan. Only to take it away, far away, to the river or the woods. To bury the guilt and the fear. Deep.

The morning was already hot. In the village paint had blistered on the doorways; a dog slept on the warm cobbles of The Bull yard. A few early cars slurred down the road; a milkvan whirred in Cross Street.

He paused at the excavation. It was the first time he had been back there; the devastation had been tidied up, and it looked fairly normal. This would be the easiest place, the place where it had come from, but they would find it again, too easily. On the bridge he stared down at the muddy river, falling in ebb. Still too close.

Deliberately, he headed away from Belin's Hill. The heavy ramparts, dark with oaks, rose in the sky behind him, but he turned his back, towards the lanes, the outlying ridge of Wentwood. He climbed to it through fields, scattering discontented cows, over gates and stiles, deep into the wood. It rose up around him all at once, so that there were no horizons, and the rich smell of the trees closed him in. Deep among leaves and bracken he stumbled, keeping the sun in front of him, walking far into the great forest.

He was hot by now, and thirsty, but he would not stop. The sack was heavy; anxiously he scuffed aside leaves and slid into hollows, poked into rabbit-holes and the boles of trees, but there was nowhere big enough or deep enough. The ground was baked hard and he had nothing to dig with. Sitting for a minute on a fallen beech he rubbed sweat from his face and waved gnats away. A spade. He should have brought one. But it would have been too heavy.

He ate some dry biscuits and an orange and looked down at the hated sack. He was tempted to leave it here; just to cover it up and go. But he knew it wouldn't be enough. And he had to be sure.

Half an hour later, he came to the cutting. From the top, he stared down with a mixture of fear and relief; a deep scar through the wood, littered with the fallen leaves of decades, its sides overgrown with bracken and thorn and small sprouting saplings of oak.

Climbing down carefully, slipping on the loose soil, he told himself that this was the place. There was nothing here to hurt him, no trains, not on this line. It had been closed for years; even at the bottom there was no sign of a track or sleepers, just the forest, smelling of sap, the thick stems snapping and splintering as he waded through them. And ahead of him, as he almost had known it would be, was the tunnel.

It had been boarded up, but the forest had splintered through. Rotting planks and corrugated iron sheets peeled among the brambles; behind a curtain of ferns and hanging weeds a huge black hole opened in the hillside.

Huw paused. All his instincts, all his nightmares broke out in him, but he forced himself to be calm, to ignore them, to think! Where better than here? No one would ever find it.

It took him about five minutes to gather up the courage. It was harder than he had thought possible, but he shouldered the sack and forced his way in.

Chest-high, the bracken was green and soft; disturbed butterflies drifted up from it. Tugging at a rotten corner of wood, he had to leap back as a whole section crushed and fell into dust, blinding him, its echoes thundering under the hill.

For a long, unbearable moment it sounded like a train, and his whole body ached to run.

He held himself still, gasping, almost sobbing. He was afraid of the tunnel, of the memories it brought back, of the endless crashing of metal. But he was more afraid of the head.

He picked up the sack and moved on, into the tunnel.

It was black; rank with the earth-smell. After only a few steps in he was blind as a mole, chilled with damp that plopped in the silence. It was cold in here. He had almost forgotten how good that felt, but the darkness breathed about him, dripping; something slid and fell from the roof. He crouched quickly, jabbing at the invisible soil with a jagged piece of metal from outside. It was important not to imagine. Just to get this done, and get out.

He drove the rough edge down; it was powdery and sharp in his hot, filthy fingers, and cut easily into the damp soil. He scraped and dug and scraped again, gasping in the silence. Beneath him, in the dark, the hole grew. The pit. He felt its depth, scooping the soft soil out with his fingers, dragging it away, plunging his arm in up to the shoulder.

It felt deep, deep enough; he crammed the sack inside, pushing it down, and to his momentary delight it seemed to settle, to sink, and he piled armfuls of earth onto it, stones and debris, trampling it down, covering it with broken bricks and wood dragged from the entrance.

Then there was nothing in his hands. It was gone.

Breathless he crouched, coughing in the damp. The echoes faded. Gradually the silence of the tunnel encircled him, and a sudden darkness.

He raised his head, abruptly.

In the green sunlight of the tunnel arch someone was standing. A tall shape, blurred in the haze.

'Hal?' he murmured.

Damp plipped in the dark.

The figure came closer. It wavered, almost dissolving in the brambles and nettles, the sun-glare. He caught a glimpse of its eyes, briefly.

Squirming back, Huw felt the whole empty tunnel yawn behind him. Draughts stirred in it; it led deep into the earth. He stood still, afraid to go back.

'Who are you?' he murmured, and the tunnel caught the words and whispered them, over and over, down the miles of emptiness behind him.

Who are you? Who are you?

CHAPTER 14

Hal came down the steps and looked around. He saw a stone bench, sun-warm, in one corner; behind it a rose bush clipped and pruned to neatness, the deep crimson flowers burning. Underfoot, on the cracked paving, there were no weeds, only the thick soft cushions of moss that Lizzie hadn't had the heart to pull up. There were little walls and stone ornaments that he hadn't seen for years.

For a moment he stared at the emerging garden, then turned to look down over the valley. Heat-haze hid the river; even the rooftops of the village were lost in it. While the shadow inched over the sundial like a dark finger, he watched it, rubbing sweat from his forehead.

The valley was drying up. He thought of the scorched fields, the cracking, shrivelled river-banks. A butterfly settled on his arm, but he didn't notice. There was no wind, no sound. The house and the haze below were silent as a deserted dream, wrapped in long veils of light, and a sombre, brooding unease.

Sunglare burned his neck, the back of his hands, the garden trembling like a mirage. He stood up, quickly, and walked down the terrace.

Lizzie and Phil were trying to heave up a ragged clump of hemlock, sneezing and giggling as the thick stems sent clouds of white fluffy seed drifting around them.

'Sorry about the mess,' Lizzie gasped, seeing him.

Phil sat weakly on a wall. 'We can't shift it,' he said, holding his side. 'It's older than I am!'

'Where's Huw?' Hal asked quietly.

Phil glanced at Lizzie.

'He went out early,' she said. 'Before breakfast.'

'Where?'

'He didn't say. There was no one up.' There was an edge of worry in her voice. They both noticed it.

'He'll turn up,' Phil muttered, picking fluff out of his hair. Hal said nothing. He pulled a leaf to pieces in moody silence.

Phil pulled a face at her. They both knew there had been some sort of row last night. Phil thought that Hal had caught Huw exploring in the house, and had lost his temper. 'He's been a bit quiet lately,' he murmured.

Hal looked up. 'Has he said anything to you?'

'What about?'

For a moment Hal looked uneasily at them. 'Things.' He shrugged. 'I can't tell you. It's up to Huw. He should.'

Lizzie said, 'What's wrong, Hal?'

'The heat,' he muttered, looking away, and she knew it

was the truth, but that he meant something else by it, something worse. He knew something, and in a sharp moment of understanding she realised it was dangerous, and that Huw was caught up in it; how pale he was these days, how tense.

'It's not his mind,' Hal looked up, abruptly. 'When he tells you, don't think that. I know he's had that injury but it's not that. This is real. He's trying not to believe it, but he will.'

He stepped back but she following him, catching his arm. 'What's real? You have to tell me what's going on.'

Her hand was hot; gently he pulled away. Then he said, 'I can't, Lizzie. I promised I wouldn't. He needs to tell you himself.' He turned away, then back, quickly. 'You weren't in the train with them, were you?'

'I was here.' The sudden question took her off guard.

'Could you tell me about it?'

Phil shot him a glare but Lizzie nodded, slowly, playing with the end of her hair. 'If it helps. Huw, Mam and Dad were coming home after a weekend in London. It derailed, in the tunnel. Huw doesn't talk about it, ever, but when they found him he was partly clear of the wreckage.' Her voice was bleak. 'It took a long time to get him out. Hours.'

Hal nodded. 'I'm sorry,' he said, and she knew he meant this, and other things, but before she could answer she saw fear, surprising and unmistakable, come into his eyes. He glanced round. 'Did you hear that?'

'What?'

He didn't answer, listening hard. Then he said, 'Lizzie, I want you to leave the garden. Leave it alone.'

'After all our work?' Phil was outraged.

'I'm sorry. It's just that the house . . . I can't let all that be woken up. It's too dangerous.'

Lizzie stared at him. She went up one step, her red hair gleaming in the hot light. 'Do you just want the house to fall down, Hal? Not even one stone on another? Because that's what will happen, if—'

'Then let it,' he said suddenly, interrupting. 'Let it.'

His anger silenced her. Not until he was halfway up the steps did she speak again and then she said, quietly, 'I did hear something.'

He turned. 'What?'

'Someone laughing. A woman.'

He nodded, briefly. Then he walked into the house.

Through the arch of sunlight Huw could see smoke. It crackled out there in the wood; he could hear the snap and spit of it, and he coughed as it swirled through the tunnel.

The figure waited, blurred in the edges of light.

'Leave me alone!' Huw let the tunnel mumble the words. They rose to a strange meaningless rumble; he pulled himself up and stood, one step from the wall.

The man had a hand on the brick entrance; he was bent, as if staring in. He asked something, an echoing question. Huw stumbled forward over the broken bricks and rusting metal sheets. Smoke stung his eyes; he felt the whole tunnel shudder, as if, far away a train was coming, screeching over points, rumbling in the blackness of the earth.

'No,' he muttered. 'There's no train. No danger.'

The man backed from the tunnel entrance, and behind him, to Huw's astonishment, the pillar of stone stood in the wood. Askew, tipped to one side, the grey column glimmered in the sunlight, ivy masking its base. And balanced on the top, looking at him, was the stone head.

Its eyes were blank and intense. Taints of power shimmered in the air around it; it crackled with heat in the dry clearing, tingling his nerves and fingers even from here.

Huw stared at it, sick with despair. He knew it was an illusion; the head was buried behind in the tunnel, in the dark, and he willed the thing to be gone, to stop haunting him, and as he forced it to go it went, shimmering out, fading, until there was nothing there.

With a hiss of delight Huw stepped nearer the sunlight.

'Now you!' he snapped.

The figure turned to him, came closer, blurred.

'Huw!' it said, urgently.

Sun broke in his eyes, making them water.

His father was looking at him.

A small, wiry man; a man wearing jeans and that old red rugby shirt. For a second, in absolute silence, Huw saw him clearly; his amazement was so great that he felt it rumble round him, it shook the tunnel so that dust crashed. A board slithered, smacking down, and the sound grew and thundered, shaking the ground under his feet. Far back, deep in the hill's darkness, the train was coming. It roared through hillsides, through all the tunnels and cuttings in his head, through the pores and veins and hollows of his body. The train was in him, it had always been in him! Louder it came, it was his blood, his fear, and his father's voice was shouting somewhere. Nightmare broke out around him, the oil-smell, the spinning wheels.

He picked himself up, was running, stumbling; around him the roof came crashing down, stones bouncing from his shoulders. With a cry he fell and scrambled up. The dusty hole of sunlight blurred; his father called him and he ran to him through nettles, through the crumbling bricks that slid and crashed about him, through the bracken into sunlight, into a wave of heat.

Dust spilled out after him, rolling in a great cloud. The tunnel collapsed, with an endless thunder of noise. The clearing in the wood was empty.

Coughing, he ran down the cutting until his breath gave out; then he leaned, hands against a tree, watching the dust settle, the rumble of falling rock die slowly down. Rumble after rumble, then a slither of soil. Then silence.

He breathed deep. Dust drifted in the sunlight.

Slowly, the giddiness ebbed. A blackbird flew back and sang a few notes, not far off in the wood. Huw opened his eyes, and looked back.

The tunnel mouth gaped. Half-blocked with rubble, it breathed dust into the warm air.

But where the pillar of stone had stood was something still; a faint shadow on the air, like the echo of a face.

CHAPTER 15

'Can I go into the church?'

The vicar, splashing washing-up water on the parched lawn, looked up in surprise.

'Huw!' he said genially. 'What happened to you last night?'

'I went home early.'

'Are you all right?'

'Fine thanks.' Huw kicked the crisp weeds at the gate.

No, you're not, Mitchel thought. Far too pale for one thing. 'Of course you can go in,' he said aloud. 'Any time. It's never locked. After a bit of piece and quiet, eh?'

'Somewhere cool.'

'Oh, it's like a fridge in there.' He put the blue bowl under his arm and said, 'You were asking about those clay heads. I've got them here, if you want to take a look.'

Huw turned a look on him; a look so strange that it worried him.

'No. No. I've seen enough.'

He watched the boy vanish into the churchyard.

Something was wrong there, very wrong. Ever since that business in Cross Street, at least. Perhaps a word with Tom Griffiths might be worthwhile. He flipped the washing-up bowl over, thoughtfully, scattering the last few drops of water on the dusty soil. They soaked in instantly, uselessly.

The church was very quiet as Huw came in, the roof high and cool. Long shafts of sunlight slanted through the upper windows, spilling bright diamonds down the opposite wall.

Halfway up the aisle he slipped into a bench behind a pillar of white stone. It was peaceful here; he leaned his head back in relief. All the way back through the wood, this had been the only place he could think of. A place that would be safe. It was cool here, and so quiet. He drew his feet up and hugged them, listening to the creaking of the roof, an ice-cream van chiming in the street outside.

He could have been killed.

He thought of his father, that glimpse. It had been such a relief, such a shock. It warmed him to think of it. 'Thank you,' he said aloud, very quietly. The church hummed the words, like a murmur of voices.

Whatever it was out there, it was hunting him, deliberately. He felt as if he was on the run from it, hiding in corners. Nowhere was safe. It could get into his dreams even, into his mind. He knew now he would have to tell Lizzie, and maybe Phil – yes, both of them. But what? About the excavation. About the head. Something was alive here; he had brought it to life and he had to find out what it wanted. And he was sick of struggling with it all on his own.

He closed his eyes, feeling the sweat drying on his back. He'd been up hours already, and the sleepless nights were catching up with him. After a moment, he huddled up on the hard bench and put his head on his arm.

Before he was comfortable, he was asleep.

Hal cut the soft vase off the wheel and crumpled it up. He squeezed the clay with one hand into a tangled, kneaded mess. Then he flung it irritably into the clay-bin.

At the door, the dog looked up at him.

Running his sticky fingers through his hair, Hal sat in silence. Flies buzzed in the workshop; the lavender bush just outside the door scorched the air with scent.

He was hot, and tired, and beyond all that, he was scared. For nights now the ghost of the woman had wandered the house, her low laugh waking him so that he lay still for hours, imagining the stiff rustle of her dress in the deserted corridors. He knew she had begun to work on him, as she had with all of them, his father, his grandfather, all the troubled generations. Night after night now she would torment him with fear; the menace of her would tangle round the house. She would never leave him alone.

He stood up, abruptly, stepped over the sleepy dog and went through the courtyard to the back of the house, into the kitchens. They were vast, and empty. A tiny fridge stood alone in one corner; he rummaged in there and found nothing to drink, slamming the door in quiet anger.

A pottery mug stood on the wooden draining-board; he filled that with cold water from the only tap and drank, thirstily, looking round. Great iron spits hung from chains, rusting under the huge throat of the chimney. Soot had fallen in there, and an old crow's nest from last winter. He gazed at it, unseeing. There was nothing to eat, either, though he wasn't hungry. He knew he was letting things slip. But the village had become a place of gossip and mockery, of suspicious eyes and smirking behind his back. He had to force himself to go down there.

And this morning, he should have told Lizzie, warned her, said something, because Huw was caught up in this, and he didn't understand why, understand any of it. Except that the danger was growing. That was certain.

And if only it would rain.

He put the mug down and wandered upstairs, through the empty rooms and corridors where the wallpaper hung limp and damp. His footsteps echoed; the clock in the library tocked loudly through the hush. Outside the house the hot afternoon sweltered, the sky a deep, unbroken blue, the tips of the leaves turning crisp.

He glanced up at Rowena's portrait, but the coldness of her smile chilled him and he walked out again, restlessly, up the wide curving staircase to the bedrooms.

121

Halfway, he stood still.

Above him, a door had slid shut.

Something snapped in him then, a fury that hurt like a pain in his chest. He sprinted up the stairs. At the top he listened, intent.

These were the attics; he rarely came up here. Dust furred the floor; the plasterwork had fallen all down one corridor, exposing the bare lathes. Angrily, he stalked between the closed doors.

Ahead, in the dimness, something was creaking, rhythmic and clear. At the fourth door he paused to listen, then turned the handle and flung it wide, letting it bang against the inner wall.

She would choose this room.

The window had broken; over the years ivy had grown inside, a mass of it down the wall. Grotesquely it sprawled on the nursery wallpaper, glossy leaves tapping in the warm air, staining the faded blue ABC blocks that he knew so well.

Unmoving, he watched the chair.

It rocked slowly, back and forth, as if she was still sitting there, facing him, invisible. But it was rotten. Spars had snapped from the back; one armrest hung useless.

Hal stood still. This had been his own bedroom, years ago, the place where he had hidden from the fear of the disturbed house. The great key still stuck out of the rusty lock.

He came in.

The room stank of mildew, its floorboards rotten and dangerous. Crossing them carefully, he put one hand on the chair and stopped it, feeling the pressure. In front of him a breeze rustled the leaves. Suddenly it felt like a trap.

'Where are you?' he murmured.

A bird fluttered in the window, catching his eyes, and he saw deep among the leaves a face looking back at him, reflected in a broken pane, a narrow face, dark and lost. For a moment he saw himself, mirrored between the ivy leaves; then the window banged with a slam that made him jump; glass slid and tinkled on the floor, a shiver of disintegrating light.

Something touched his hand.

He jerked back with a gasp; grabbed for the door and stumbled back out of the room.

A murmur of amusement followed him; like a draught it touched his hair and face, and with a cry of terror he beat her off, moving back to the stairs, fear pulsing in him, until he stopped and gripped the banister. Before him the corridor was empty.

'Leave me alone,' he gasped, and then he shouted it, so that the house rang. 'Leave me alone!'

She came for him, all the malice of her, the mockery. Shadows and sunlight glinted; smoke hung in the spaces, a red flamelick that rippled on walls and doors. Something reached out for him, scratched at him. He squirmed back and twisted away, slipped and crashed down, stair after stair, flung with abrupt pain against the wall at the bottom.

Dizzy and breathless, struggling up, he dragged in air, doubled over. Blood ran down his face; astonished, he wiped it on the dirty white sleeve of his shirt.

From somewhere above, the darkness laughed at him.

Holding the wall, struggling to breathe, he knew that she would hunt him down, break up his mind. Then she would kill him.

As she had killed all the rest.

When Huw woke he was stiff and bewildered, not sure where he was. He sat up.

Far down at the end of the aisle, through the red piece of glass in Rowena's window, someone was watching him. Odd hysterical thoughts came to him. How he must look, here on the bench, tiny in the distance.

And the church had been cool before but it was cold now, cold as a tomb, and the sweaty sleeve of his shirt was ice and it ached his arm.

He got up and ran, down the aisle, across the porch, through the great wooden doors. Warm air embraced him like a muffling blanket. He bolted round the corner and ran the length of the churchyard through the long grass, churning clouds of pollen into the sticky air. Then he flung himself around the east wall and stopped, heart pounding.

There was no one there.

After a few seconds he went and stood behind the window. Carefully, he stretched up and put his eye to the fire-red piece of glass. He could see the aisle, and the pillar, and, as red as if it burned in some inferno, the bench where he had been sitting, halfway down.

CHAPTER 16

John Mitchel leaned back in his armchair and sipped the iced beer. It had been a long, scorching day.

The doors to the garden were open; even now the evening was hot, filling the room with the scents of phlox and roses and lavender. He was worn out with trying to keep them watered, he thought, leaning his head back. A thrush began to sing creamily down the garden; he thought about a cigarette, and the TV news.

The cigarette won. As he reached for his jacket the clock pinged nine, and the door opened.

'I'm just off,' his housekeeper said, putting on her cardigan. 'And there's a visitor for you. Mr Vaughn.' She raised her eyebrows, meaningfully.

The vicar struggled up from his chair. 'Hal?' They exchanged looks of surprise. 'Send him in, Siân.'

As she went out he lit the cigarette and clicked the lighter off. What would Hal want? He rarely came to the house.

When Hal came in the dog padded behind him as

usual. 'This is a bit of a surprise,' the vicar said, sarcastically. 'Sit down. Drink?'

'No thanks.' Hal sat wearily on the couch in the corner; the same place that Huw had lain. The dusty cherubs watched him from the ceiling. The room was dim with a rosy evening light; the vicar clicked the lamp on.

'That's better. Now what can I do for you?' Turning, he saw Hal's face; there was a long scratch on his cheek, barely closed. He looked pale and nervous, though he was trying not to show it, wiping the dog's paws with a handkerchief.

'Sorry, John. He's been in some mud. God knows where he found it.'

The dog snuffled away among the furniture.

Struck by Hal's look, and some nagging memory he couldn't pin down, Mitchel sat by the empty fireside. 'You don't look so well. Anything wrong?'

Hal laughed, almost bitterly. He pushed his hair back from his forehead. 'Something's wrong. Badly wrong. And you know it.'

Puzzled, Mitchel said, 'You mean the weather?'

'And more.' Hal leaned forward, clenching his fingers together. 'Huw told me there have been some . . . objects, found in the village. Heads, made of clay. He said you'd got them.'

'Oh those!' The vicar blew out a cloud of smoke. 'They've been turning up all over the place. Since the dig was wrecked. Do you want to see them?'

127

He got up and crossed to an old dark-wood bureau crammed to overflowing with bills and papers; taking a key from a mug with CYMRU on it he unlocked a small cupboard and brought out a few knobbly parcels of newspaper.

'You keep it locked,' Hal said quietly.

'Yes. Don't know why, really.' Dumping the parcels on the carpet he began to unwrap one. 'Perhaps I just don't like the thought of these things down here in the night. They're a bit uncanny. This one was in the pub.'

He watched, shrewdly, but Hal showed no signs of recognition. He held out his hand for the thing and took it, reluctantly, almost as if it disgusted him, gazing at it, his face pale.

The clay head stared back, the shadows from the lamp flickering in its eyes.

'Horrible, isn't it?' Mitchel sat back on his heels. 'Vaguely malicious, I think. The others are all the same.' He laid them side by side. The room seemed dimmer, shadowed. In the hush the thrush stopped singing; a faint wind stirred the flowers.

'I showed them to Jane Matthews – that girl at the dig – and she got quite intrigued. Said they were modern copies of a –'

'Celtic stone head.' Hal stared down at the thing in his hand.

'Well that's right. Used in some religious rite, sacrifice, who knows.' Mitchel watched his guest's absorption with interest. He said quietly, 'No one knows who made them. But I've been thinking. If they are copies there must be an original. Perhaps whoever wrecked the dig has it.'

Hal looked up sharply. 'You think so?'

'Yes.' Despite himself, the vicar felt worried. He gathered the snarling, lipless faces into a pile and bundled the paper round them, thinking rapidly. Hal knew something. He'd never been so agitated before, so edgy. He was just working up to a question when Hal stood up.

'Burn those things, John. The sooner the better. There won't be any more. Come on, Mick.'

'Wait!' It burst from Mitchel in such a hurry that he surprised himself. 'Hal, wait, please. You haven't told me yet what's wrong.'

Hal stopped. They looked at each other across the dim room. Then he said slowly, 'It doesn't matter.'

'Of course it does!' Alarmed, Mitchel stood up. 'Tell me. I might be able to help. I know most of the things that go on here, after all.'

Hal almost smiled. 'I know you do.'

'Have you been ill?'

'No.' The dark eyes watched him, as if Hal was measuring him up, wondering whether to trust him. 'I haven't been sleeping too well.'

Uneasy, the vicar laughed. 'The heat? Or a guilty conscience?'

Hal said nothing.

The vicar fumbled with his cigarette, looking for an ashtray. 'I just wish you'd talk to me, that's all.'

With sudden ferocity Hal leaned forward. 'You think it was me, don't you?'

'Of course I don't.'

'You think I wrecked the excavation and made these things. For God's sake, John! I thought I could trust you, at least!'

Rueful, the vicar sat down. 'I'm sorry,' he said at last. 'I have to admit the thought crossed my mind.'

'You and a hundred others.'

'It was stupid of me. I'm sorry.'

Hal stood near the door, but didn't move; his fingers gripping the frayed back of the couch. There was an awkward silence. The clock ticked; outside, the twilight darkened. Not knowing what else to do, the vicar stubbed out his cigarette and lit another.

'Those things stink,' Hal muttered.

Shaking out the match, Mitchel nodded. 'You get so used to it.'

Slowly, Hal came back. He perched on the edge of the sofa wearily. 'All right. I'll try to explain. You won't believe all of it, but it's serious. The proof is there in those paper parcels.' He took a deep breath. 'It wasn't me who wrecked the dig. It was Huw.'

'Good Lord,' the vicar said thoughtfully.

'You knew?'

'I had a feeling he knew something about it. But go on.'

130

'I don't know how to.' Quickly, Hal explained about the head, how Huw had dragged it from the earth. Mitchel was appalled.

'The boy's a vandal!'

'You don't understand. It . . . made him.'

'It?'

Looking out of the window, Hal nodded. 'I think it began again that day with the car. Something woke up, deep in the earth. It's haunting him. It wants something. I'm afraid of what it might make him do.'

The vicar shook his head, bemused. 'I thought he'd been looking a bit peaky. But haunting? Look, Hal, he's just lost his parents. He's been in hospital with head injuries. That could explain a lot of this.'

'Yes, but I haven't.'

'You?' The vicar glanced up in surprise.

Hal was watching him closely. 'I've heard things, John, felt things. In the house. She's come back.'

'She?'

'You know who I mean. The house has been quiet for years, since my father . . . I'd hoped it might stay that way. But she's back, in all the rooms, in the corridor, every night . . .'

'What have you heard?'

'Noises. Doors. She laughs, sometimes. She scratched my face.'

He stood up and went to the garden door, looking out. Mitchel stared at his back. He had no idea what to say.

Tapping his cigarette on the ashtray he murmured, 'You could move out. It's too lonely living up there. Get a room in the village. You could stay here, I've got a spare room.'

'It's not the house!' Hal didn't turn, but the vicar sensed his tension. 'My great-grandfather left the house. He died abroad. It doesn't make any difference. It's the family she haunts! The people.'

'That word again.'

Hal turned. 'What word?'

'Haunts. Look, Hal . . .' he laughed, unhappily. 'I may be a minister of the church but I'm not sure if I . . . well, not ghosts. It's not that I don't believe you, it's just that I don't –'

'You think I'm imagining it.' Hal gazed at him sourly. 'Talk to Huw, John. That's all I want you to do.'

'I'll have a go, if you think it will help.'

'I do.'

'I'll go up tomorrow, if I've got time.' Mitchel stood up, smiling. 'And in the meantime, Hal, go home and get some sleep. It's this weather that's getting us all down. I'm sure things are not as bad as you think.'

Hal stood in the doorway for a moment, unmoving. Then he said, 'Goodnight, John.'

When he was gone, out through the twilit garden, the vicar came back and stood for a while, caught by his own slanted reflection in the open door. Then he sat in the armchair and took another cigarette from the packet. Tapping it on the box impatiently, he knew that he hadn't said enough. He had failed. Hal had come for some sort of help and he hadn't even been able to believe him. But ghosts . . .?

He crumpled the cigarette up slowly, and threw it into the bin.

CHAPTER 17

Late that night Lizzie was jerked out of sleep. She opened her eyes and sat up. The echo of a great noise hung in the room; a moment ago it had been loud; near and sudden.

She listened.

Branches against the window, tiles creaking. Nothing else. The silent green dial of her clock said twenty past two. She sat still for a while, leaning back on the pillow, sinking back into sleep. There were only the three of them in the house tonight; Phil's parents were away. Or maybe they'd come back. Maybe it had been the car door slamming.

A scratch at the open window; then another.

She opened her eyes.

Quietly at first, muffled, the sounds began outside. She sat up and listened, her heart thumping. What was it? Murmurs and scrapes. Stiff, metallic sounds, like huge hard beetle-wings scraping up the wall.

She swung her legs out and crossed, quickly, to the window, pulling back a corner of the gauzy curtain and peering out. No car. A bright moon poured its brilliance into the yard, distorting shadows. The sounds came from further along, under the trees by Huw's window; she thought she heard a voice, and caught a dark movement in the shadows.

She stared at it. Someone was there, standing so still, blending with the apple-boles so she could hardly make him out. But he was there, and up on Belin's Hill were tiny flares like fires, high in the mass of oaks.

Suddenly the dog howled, round in the barn; so horrible a noise that she leapt back in fright. A small vase wobbled and fell, smashing to shards of glass.

She swore, grabbed a dressing-gown and ran out onto the landing, straight into Phil.

'What is it?' she hissed.

'The wretched dog. Rats, I expect.' But he sounded uneasy, and came with her as she knocked on Huw's door, quietly at first, then louder.

Anxiously, she pushed it open.

The room was dark. Huw was standing by the window, a tousle-haired silver-white figure. When he realised they were there he slammed the window down and spun around. Instantly, the sounds stopped.

He ran over and pushed them out of the room. 'Come on, quick!'

'Where?'

'Downstairs. No wait . . . First shut all the windows up here. Quickly! Do they lock?'

'I expect so,' Phil said blankly 'but –'

'Just lock them!' And Huw was gone, racing downstairs.

'Better do it,' Lizzie said, worried.

Phil stared at her. 'Is he all right?'

'I don't know.' Tired, she shook her head. 'I think something's wrong. Hal tried to say as much.'

Phil went into his room, slammed the window and locked it. As they ran down they could hear Huw jamming the thick, squeaky bolts across the kitchen door.

The kitchen was in total darkness, with only a silver line of moonlight that sliced the floor, and the flicker of a candle Huw had stuck hastily onto the fridge. Lizzie caught it as it toppled; Huw shoved past her, testing the windows, banging tight the old shutters that had been unused since the war.

'Huw!' Phil stared at him in disbelief. 'What's going on! Why no lights?'

'They don't work, that's why.'

Lizzie flicked the switch. 'He's right.'

Huw was at the back door; he began to push the heavy kitchen table towards it. 'Help me with this.'

'What?'

He turned, his face white and strained. 'Help me, Phil! Now!'

For a moment Phil hesitated. Then he leaned against one end of the table and the three of them jammed it against the back door, firmly. Huw stepped back, breathless, but Phil caught his arm.

'I want to know what's going on, now!' His voice was harsh and urgent. 'Who's outside? What do they want? The place looks like a fortress.'

'It is a fortress.' Huw pulled away, not looking at them. He knew this was the time. 'That noise . . . the dog. He can feel them out there.'

Lizzie sat down on a chair. 'Them?' she whispered.

'It. I don't know.'

Phil stared at them both in horror. 'You mean someone might hurt him? Rex?' He turned and began to pull hurriedly at the table, heaving it away from the door. Huw was behind him at once. 'Stop it! Where are you going?'

'To get the dog.'

'It doesn't want the dog!' Almost frantic with despair Huw hauled him away. 'It's not a man out there, not a person, haven't you realised that yet? It's . . . a thing, a power . . . I don't know what to call it!' Shaking now, almost crying, he stumbled back through the moonlight. 'And it doesn't want the dog, or you, or Lizzie. It wants me. Only me!'

A tremendous crash made them all jump.

The kitchen door shuddered heavily. The table in front of it leapt forward with the sudden vibration. Without hesitating, the three of them shoved it back, leaned against it, hearts pounding.

They waited.

It was quiet for a few seconds. Nobody spoke. On the fridge the candle guttered.

Then, just as Lizzie began to breathe again, a great crack shattered the silence. Glass tinkled. Pane by pane they heard it smash and fall from the windows; crashing in sheets, sliding down the walls outside, window after window until they thought it would never stop.

Fear pushed them back, slowly, against the dresser. Then Lizzie caught Huw's arm. 'Look!' she breathed.

On the furthest window, the shutters were bending.

They bent inwards, straining under the force of some enormous strength, splintering, creaking slowly apart. Dark splits appeared in the wood, lengthened, shot upwards. With a yell of terror Huw ran out and flung himself against them, trying desperately to push it back, hold it out, stop it getting in; wildly he realised he was shouting in blind panic; then Phil hauled him back, and yelled at him fiercely to shut up.

There was silence.

A fragment of glass slid out and shattered.

No sound came from outside.

Huw was shaking; he tried to stop. He felt cold and hot at once; sick and shaky with panic. He sat down, got up, didn't know what he was doing; suddenly he felt desolate, and lost, utterly lost.

'Liz?' he sobbed.

'Over here.' She came and caught hold of him, taking

him to the corner by the fridge. 'It's all right,' she said. She sounded like his mother.

'I'm sorry,' he whispered. 'This is all my fault.'

For a while they waited, afraid to move. Then as the silence lengthened and the moonlight crept over the floor, they sat in a huddle against the dresser, all together.

'Is it still there?' Lizzie whispered, her arm round Huw.

'Something is.' Phil moved closer, till they could see the edge of his face and the blue of the jumper he had pulled on upstairs. 'Come on, Huw,' he said quietly. 'Let's hear it.'

Huw fixed his eyes on the door, shuddering. It was hard to get the words out. 'It's my fault. I was the one who broke into the dig.'

'You?' Phil stared; then he shook his head. 'But why?'

'I don't know why.' Huw shuddered again; through her arm Lizzie felt it. 'I had a dream; as if I was sleepwalking. As if it took me over. I went down there. I dug up this thing, this stone head.' As he described it they stared at him in horror; he told them about how he had tried to get rid of it, the way it kept coming back. Then he told them about the tunnel.

'And you went inside?' Lizzie sounded half-admiring. 'After all that's happened?'

'I had to. I didn't know what else to do.' He felt weary now, drained, washed clean. Telling it all was an enormous relief. 'Do you believe me?' he murmured.

They looked at each other. Phil shrugged.

'Hal told us to believe you,' Lizzie said.

'He knows,' Huw said uneasily. 'He's in this too. That woman, Rowena.'

'But the curse is on his family, not yours.'

'I know.'

The candle had been guttering; now it went out and left them in darkness.

'Any more?' Lizzie whispered.

Phil pulled out a drawer, and began to rummage through it. 'I don't think so.'

Huw stared at the shaft of moonlight. 'What can I do, Liz?'

She pulled her dressing-gown round her and frowned in the dark. 'We have to think clearly. It doesn't seem to have any real power over you. It can't get into the house.'

'It might have already. Upstairs . . .'

'We'd have heard it,' she said firmly, blotting out a sudden vivid picture in her mind of a man's hands groping over the sill of a window. 'And you've got rid of the head . . .'

'It's hunting me. It wants me to do something!'

'Then perhaps we should find out what.'

He stared at her, appalled. At the same time Phil crouched down. 'Look at the window.'

The long silver stream of light was blotted out, as if a dark shape stood outside; they heard a movement at the shutter, a scratch.

Lizzie got up. She moved a step or two closer.

'Don't!' Phil hissed.

But in the dimness they saw her figure close to the window.

'Who are you?' she whispered. 'What do you want?'

They waited for an answer. No one spoke.

Then the moonlight broke out again across the room.

'It's gone,' Phil breathed.

'Maybe.'

They waited in the dark room, uneasy, unwilling to speak. Minutes crept to hours; the silver finger of moonlight wandered across the wall and vanished, leaving them wrapped in a warm blackness with only the green light on the fridge by the door. Sometimes they dropped into sleep, jerked awake by the bang of a gate outside, or unexplained shuffles round the walls of the house.

Late in the night, Huw dozed against Lizzie's shoulder, and dreamed that the walls of the house melted away and the forest broke in. Huge gnarled oak trees sprouted up from the floor, smashing through tiles and jagged, splintered floorboards, their roots winding tight about the legs of chairs, about Lizzie, and Phil. He thought he sat up and began to tug at the growth and the weeds, snapping them frantically, tearing them out of Lizzie's hair. But the weeds still grew, and under them was a mass of rotting leaves, stinking of decay, and a pit, that opened down and down into the hot darkness. He slid, gripping a tangle of bindweed, but his hands were hot and sweaty and they slipped, and he fell, down and down and down into the dark until someone jerked his arm and he opened his eyes.

'Huw! Wake up! I thought you said you'd buried that head thing?'

Bewildered, he struggled up. 'I did.'

'Well come and see.'

The back door was unlocked. The morning sun, already hot, was streaming in, and Lizzie was standing in it. At her feet, on the step, was the stone head.

It was split in half, from forehead to chin, and had fallen open.

Each lidless eye glared in a different direction.

CHAPTER 18

'I can't stay here!'
Pulling on his shirt, Huw kept his face to the window. They'd had to open it, open all the windows. Already the heat was oppressive, a weight on the house.

'But, Huw . . .'

'It's not safe! They're after me. You can stay if you want . . .'

'Don't be stupid!' She grabbed him and swung him round. 'We'll come. But where? Think!'

He fought down terror, trying to get his tired memory to work. There had been somewhere. Somewhere safe. 'We have to take it –'

'To the pillar on the hill.' Phil stood in the doorway, his hair rough and uncombed. He looked bleary and anxious.

Huw stared at him for a moment. Then he said, 'Not up there. That's what it wants.'

'There's nowhere else.'

'Yes there is.' He felt calmer now; his heart had stopped thumping so much. 'We can take it to the church. I should have thought of that before.' He did up the last button and went reluctantly across the room. 'Where is it?'

Phil pulled a face. 'Downstairs. In the rucksack.' He flicked a glance at Lizzie. 'What do you think?'

She nodded, slowly. 'We have to talk to someone. The vicar will be there.'

They grabbed a hurried breakfast and left quickly; Phil with the old green rucksack over his shoulder. Huw was relieved. He couldn't bear to carry it now, even to think of it. He tried not to think of anything.

The farm was oddly quiet, the hens barely peering out, the dog cowed and silent in the yard. A shed door hung ajar; soft ripples of dust moved and gusted among the nettles and the open space behind the tractor. As Huw turned he saw the apple trees under his window, their leaves limp in the heat, the wall of the house blindingly white. Even from here he could see the marks on the wall; scratches; long, scored fingermarks, fingers stained with soil, filthy with earth.

Phil slammed the door.

In the silence it was a huge noise, a gunshot, a crack of thunder. It rang back, faintly, over the valley, and movement stirred the trees, the dark oaks on Belin's Hill. As they crossed the deserted yard each of them felt exposed, and watched.

In the lanes too, the land was silent. No birdsong, no butterflies, not even a breeze to stir the dull, languid leaves. Heat seared the air about them, flaking the farm-track to dust, scorching the grass to crisp brown patches in the baked mud. Heat was a wall they walked into, that they breathed in, choked on. The slightest movement made them sweat, the sun burning the backs of their hands, their legs and necks. Heat was a weight they carried, sapping all energy, all exertion. In a terrible sky the sun flamed; the tarmac of the road was so hot it burned the soles of their feet.

'Where is everyone?' Lizzie muttered. They passed a deserted hayfield, the grass half-cut, the harvester standing idle by the gate.

Huw shrugged, wiping his face. 'Maybe there is no one else, any more.'

She looked at Phil, who shrugged. He wore dark glasses that hid his eyes; on his back the rucksack clunked, heavily.

A haze hung over the village, and the streets were hushed, as if everyone was still asleep, or staying out of the sun. Front doors stood ajar, their paint blistered, showing glimpses of dark, flagstoned passages, and dim, shimmering mirrors. Windows gaped; in Castle Lane the moss was dead on the walls, shrivelled to knots of stringy yellow between stones that were baking to the touch. No one was about.

Avoiding the excavation, they came the long way round, up Museum Street into the High Street. On the corner they stopped dead.

'This is weird,' Phil muttered.

The High Street was deserted. Not a car, not a person. The silence was uncanny.

'Something's happened,' Lizzie breathed.

For a moment of panic they thought they were walking in a nightmare, that the power from the earth had trapped them in a lost time. Then a small boy on a bicycle zipped past them down the street.

'Hey!' Phil yelled, but the boy was gone, round the corner.

'Come on.' Huw started after him. 'Let's get to the church.'

They hurried, in the great heat, past the houses. As they crossed the door of the Priory Hotel a dreamy tinkle of music drifted out, sounding unreal in the shimmering street. White walls were blinding; the sun glared from every surface, every window was a blaze of pain. But on the corner the old pump was dripping, as it had done for years, a miraculous glint and plip of water. As they came up to it a pigeon flew down and took a sip, its wings flashing violet-green in the glare.

'Where's all the traffic?' Phil hitched the rucksack up. 'There must have been some accident. The road must be blocked. I've never seen it like this!'

Lizzie was already at the vicarage door; they saw Mitchel come out to her. 'It's the bridge,' he said. 'Haven't you heard?' Looking at Huw, he frowned. 'That reminds me. Come in and have a drink. Something cool.'

'We can't,' Huw said abruptly. 'What's wrong with the bridge?'

'Closed.' The vicar sat on his doorstep. 'The heat has cracked the foundations, or so they think. So no traffic! Nothing can get in or out! Like going back in time, isn't it?'

'Come on.' Huw turned to the church, Phil close behind.

'Lizzie.' The vicar leaned forward. 'When you've finished, I'd like to talk to Huw. Hal's been here.'

'Hal?'

The vicar shrugged slightly, rubbing dust off his shoe. 'I don't really pretend to understand, Lizzie, but Hal has an idea Huw's in some trouble. The excavation . . .'

'You know about that?'

'He told me.' The vicar glanced casually up the street, avoiding her eyes. 'I can't help wondering . . . Huw's had a bad time –'

'It's real,' she said firmly. 'Last night Phil and I saw . . . something.'

'Something?'

She didn't explain. Instead, glancing down at the church, she asked a question that surprised him. 'What exactly happened to Hal's father?'

Mitchel stared. Finally, he said, 'It was all before my time.'

'But you know.'

He laughed, wryly. 'Of course I know. The Vaughns

have a history of being very unstable. It seems Tom Vaughn had delusions, some sort of paranoia, I suppose. He saw things, heard voices. In the end he hardly knew anyone. And now Hal's talking about ghosts . . .'

She looked at him, astonished. 'You should believe him. You're his friend.'

'I've tried, Lizzie. It's just that . . . I'm not sure.'

She turned away, almost angrily.

'Bring Huw back. Let's talk about it,' he urged.

She nodded, tight-lipped. Then she ran down the street after the others.

They were at Rowena's window.

Phil had the rucksack in his hands; he put it on the narrow shelf of the window. 'There?'

'Anywhere,' Huw muttered. He turned his back and walked straight out; they followed him. From the church door they looked towards the bridge; it was closed off with orange and white cones, loops of tape. Just visible, a large notice said:

BRIDGE CLOSED TO ALL TRAFFIC.
UNSTABLE STRUCTURE

'Unstable,' Huw muttered. 'That's what I thought I was. But it's real. It wants me and I can't get out. It wants to keep me here. And it's so hot; so hot I can't breathe.'

He was so close to despair that Lizzie grabbed his hands.

'Don't get worked up. Nothing can hurt you now. Think, Phil, where can we go? Somewhere quiet. Out of the heat.'

148

He thought a moment, then he said, 'Sor brook. Behind the village. No one goes there. But the vicar . . .'

'Forget the vicar. He won't believe us. Come on.'

The path to the Sor led behind the houses, under Belin's Hill; a hushed, hidden place, deep in trees – beeches that spread long smooth limbs out to shade the banks. The brook itself ran below them, shrunken but still rippling, and they sank down thankfully into the grass, watching the long green streamers of weed drift in the current.

Phil stretched out in the shade, eyes closed, and after a moment Lizzie took off her sandals and waded into the warm shallow water.

Huw lay listlessly on the bank, watching her. The sense of some great danger still tormented him, some dark thing gathering over him like shadow. He glanced round, uneasily. The trees were still and silent. He could not relax, but forced himself to lie back, close his eyes, feeling the rough crisp grass prickle his burned neck. Somewhere near was a smell of mint – Lizzie must have crushed some by the stream – vivid and sharp, it made him think of home, of his mother in the kitchen, chopping it on a smooth wooden board. He had not let himself think of her for so long, not of how they used to be, before the train. It hurt; half of him wanted to forget. But he forced himself to hold onto the picture, though even as he tried it was lost, and he was hearing the screech of brakes in the tunnel, feeling the coat on his lap as he pulled a packet of sweets from his pocket, seeing her face as she turned to the aisle and said, 'Can you smell smoke?'

She had turned away from him to look, and it had all happened. The world had broken open, crashed and shattered and re-formed, all wrong, all changed, like a jigsaw with pieces missing. Black gaps. Sometimes he thought the Huw who had gone into that tunnel had never come out of it.

Silence moved in the wood.

He sat up, uneasily, and turned towards the hill, as much of it as he could see; the dark shadowy ridge brooding above them.

'Something's wrong,' he murmured.

Lizzie looked over. 'It's all right.'

'No it isn't.'

Phil sat up too. He took his sunglasses off and looked around. The same feeling had come on them all, at once, the feeling Huw had known for days, of being watched, of a strange evil that was close, in the leaves, among the trees. Lizzie turned in a circle, gazing. The air was hot and sultry, the sounds they had heard vaguely for hours suddenly sharper; the wood full of rustles and scratches and mysterious quavers of bird-warning. And far down among the trees, where trunks and boles and branches meshed into greenery and shadow, they seemed to see quivers and flickers of light, barely there, unsettling.

Huw stood up.

The forest crisped; heat curled it. Tiny sputters of sizzles teased him, a haze drifted above, masking the hillside. Heat lay in the air like a heavy weight.

'What is it?' Lizzie whispered. She was close behind him, her shoes in her hand.

In the wood, something slid. Soft crackles rasped the leaves.

'Can you smell smoke?' Huw breathed.

'What?'

'Smoke. God, Lizzie! Look at the forest!'

High in the branches grey drifts blurred the sky. Small red quivers burned; a branch crashed, and far off, another.

In the trees flames burst out rippling, an edge of fire.

Tinder-dry, the wood blazed.

CHAPTER 19

The forest burned with a hissing crackle. Worms of fire ran down leaves, ate them swiftly; they blackened and charred. Among the trees the air shimmered; gusts of ash and half-burned cinder drifted down like grey snow.

Lizzie jammed on her shoes. 'How can we get back?'

'We could take a chance and run through,' Phil muttered, but even as he said it he knew it was impossible. Fire crackled and spat all around them, barely visible in the sunlight; it roared high above and a bush of elder crashed beside him suddenly, burned from root to tip.

'Phil!' Lizzie screamed, dragging him back.

'I'm all right!' He brushed ash from his face. 'It's so fast! The hill must be dry as dust.'

Behind them Huw stood rigid, unable to speak. This was his fault. All this.

'The stream.' Lizzie pushed him back, quickly. 'Get in the water!'

They plunged backwards into the narrow brook, Huw feeling it flood his shoes and splash up to this knees. But it was narrow, too narrow. And the smoke had come down around them; it hung in the roaring air, clogging their throats and eyes like fine grit, so that they coughed in ashes, and tears made pale furrows down their faces.

'Keep in the stream!' Phil grabbed Huw's sleeve. 'Work your way along. It's our only way back!'

On each side the dry bracken hissed; flames licked it away in seconds, the fronds curling, crumpling up, blackening instantly. The whole slope blurred and shimmered, its flame almost invisible, scorching up here and there in fierce, crackling implosions.

Stumbling along the narrow steam-bed, Huw felt sparks sting his arms and face; he slapped at them, yelling, staggering against Lizzie as his feet slid on the slippery, hidden stones. The air was thick with a mist of ash; it flew around them like insects, like dirty seed-fluff, swallowed, coughed up, spat out.

Hanging onto her, Huw felt Lizzie stumble; she yelled at Phil, 'Keep going! Keep going!'

Coughing, Huw glanced back, through the blurred air. He saw a tunnel of black smoke, of dim, burning shapes; stricken, he stared into his nightmare. The roof shivered, it crashed, it collapsed on him, black and hard, stunning his shoulder, flinging him down in the crusted stream. Lizzie yelled something and crouched, hauling him out; his shirt smouldered with the stink of burnt cloth.

Then sunlight flickered, burst on him.

He gasped in clean air; staggered out of Lizzie's grip

onto grass, grasping it with his hands, coughing and coughing till his chest ached.

'Look at it,' Phil's voice croaked.

The wood behind them was a sheet of flame, the blue sky awhirl with smoke.

Lizzie scrambled up the bank, weed trailing around her ankles. 'It'll reach the village!'

'It already has.'

His throat dry, Huw hauled himself up beside them. They stared at the inferno. The whole of the lower slopes of Belin's Hill were alight; a cauldron of steam. And already among the cluster of houses were flames, the roar of a smoky, quivering haze.

Huw stared at it in horror. 'The church,' he whispered.

The dog barked, once.

'Quiet,' Hal said sharply. He lay on the bench, dappled shade on his face. Then he sat up, dragging up his knees. In the sunlight the sundial leaned, a tiny growth of chickweed already greening the earth around it. Below him, the valley steamed. Heat quivered over the trees, over the distant roofs of the village.

The dog whimpered. It came out into the sun and sat looking beyond him, its long ears alert.

'What's the matter?'

He said it more gently, turning his head to the empty stairs behind him. A breeze moved the edges of leaves, one after another.

But he knew there was no breeze.

The dog backed off, whimpering, its belly down.

Hal sat still. He could see nothing, but every nerve tingled with the sense of her; he knew something was walking down the steps towards him, the hem of her dress dragging the leaves over, the soft scrape of her shoes loud in the heat.

He held himself still. All night he had sat out here and known what he had to do, had argued and tormented himself into a bitter courage. Fear broke out in him now like sweat, the cold, sickening familiar churning of his stomach, but he sat still, only the tips of his fingernails digging into the wooden seat.

The threat was close to him. It had always been close, in the house, in the family, in him. But it would end here. He said it aloud, to the rippling air. 'No one else. There won't be anyone else.'

Nothing moved; a bird called a harsh warning in the wood.

From the valley the smell of smoke rose on the hot air.

Huw was already running as fast as he could; in seconds the others raced after him, into the smoky, quivering streets. The quiet of the morning was shattered; the houses were full of shouts and people, and behind, growing louder as they ran, the ominous crackle of burning wood. Black smoke rose ahead in a great column, the harsh, acrid smell of it drifting in wisps.

They raced into the High Street, into the back of a crowd. As she shoved her way to the front someone grabbed Lizzie and held her back; wiping her eyes she saw the whole street seemed to be ablaze. The wooden fences round the excavation were burning like strips of fire. Behind them, the houses in Cross Street were being evacuated, people running out with pets and possessions under their arms. The Post Office and its adjoining cottage had great sheets of yellow flame raging out of every window. Showers of tiles and snatches of burning curtain crashed and floated down into the street, and the walls seemed to shiver through the scalding air. The crowd stood quiet, hearing the din and crash of floorboards caving in, furniture collapsing so that the flames shot higher. The heat was intense; it scorched Lizzie's face, melting the lead on the windows; tiny panes fell out, the soft metal twisting.

Then the roof of number three fell in with a terrific crash; the crowd fell back as sudden flame erupted through every gap and chink. Lizzie whirled on the woman beside her. 'Why don't they do something? Where's the fire brigade?'

'Been called, love, this half-hour. They'll have to come the long way round. The bridge is closed.'

She looked for Huw. He was watching the flames with a despairing stare; at once she hurried towards him, and the crowd shuddered and moved, crushing her, and she turned and looked up at the church. Gusts of dirty grey smoke clouded it; an ominous red glow lit the stained-glass. The street was in total confusion; people were shouting, fetching hoses, trying to organise themselves.

'Where's Huw?' Phil gasped from behind her.

'I don't know! I can't see him.'

Stumbling, shoved aside, almost frantic with a nameless dread she searched for him, pushing through the stink of smoke, the people.

Then she saw him. He had been pushed up against the railings; his eyes were fixed on the church, oblivious of the hot sparks raining around him.

Above him, Rowena's window was melting, running down into bright smears and globules of hot liquid that dripped onto the stones. The blue sky was a web of pitted cracks, the green hillside and the red piece on it softening as she watched, stretching into thick dribbles of sluggish glass, blue and green and red, twisting into coloured skeins, hanging in long pinnacles over the flames. And the words, blistered and burned and bubbled into nothing.

When she looked for Huw again he had vanished. She shouldered her way out of the crowd and ran to where Phil and the vicar were struggling with a hosepipe.

'Did you see him?'

Phil shook his head, working the valve open swiftly. She grabbed his arm, forced him to look up. 'Where is he? Has he gone up there? To the hill?'

'I don't know!' He jumped up as she turned and ran through the smoke. 'Lizzie! Wait!'

'I can't!' she yelled back. 'We don't know what he might do! Find him, Phil!' And the sparks spattered her, and she was gone.

Bewildered, Phil turned and saw the vicar watching. The harsh howl of a fire-engine echoed down the street.

'It's Huw . . .'

'I know. Wait here, Phil.'

Mitchel ran into his house. A few men dragged the hose out; water hit the flames with a great hiss and a gush of smoke. In seconds the vicar was back; he had a knobbly paper parcel under his arm, and to Phil's astonishment he ran to the burning church door and flung it in, leaping back as a fountain of sparks spat at him. For a moment he stood there, watching the blackening walls, the ashes in the hot air, and the look on his face was strange, an astonished fear, a grimness.

Then he turned.

They both ran, racing up the street, towards the great dark hill that brooded in the smoke.

CHAPTER 20

Crashing through flowers, through briars, through tall grass clouded with gnats; scrambling up into the crackle of smoke, the beat of his heart thumping like a drum, Huw flung himself up the slopes of Belin's Hill.

Ash whirled about him; through it he saw the ramparts above were huge, sometimes newly-timbered, sometimes grass-grown and worn. Bewildered, he climbed through the flickering of time, and between breaths the hill changed, wooden walls appearing and vanishing, smoke choking him, voices and whistles and stamping feet ringing round him. All the long ages the hill had known were here at once, dragging him between them, until he kept his gaze down, dizzy, fixed on the trampled grass and baked mud.

With one last effort he stumbled over the top and collapsed on his knees, gasping in air. The oaks about him wheeled in a dizzy arc. Sweat drenched his shirt; heat from the sun and the fire burned his face. Slowly he staggered up, dragging in deep breaths.

The valley seethed with smoke; a grey cover like a spun

net, hanging from hillside to hillside. Heat rose in gusts and quivers. As he stared at it a wave of fear shuddered through him at what he had done, and then abruptly, anger. It swept over him uncontrollably; anger at his parents' death, the senselessness of it, the choked-up sorrow and the empty hole in his life; anger at himself, for being always afraid; at the thing that lurked in the dark, haunting him, tormenting him.

He turned and plunged into the thicket of trees, forcing his way through so recklessly that he almost fell out into the green smooth ring of the hill-fort.

It was there.

He had known it would be.

He stared at it in fury.

Before him the pillar of stone leaned in the long grass; on the top, balanced in the hollow, the stone head looked out at him, its lopsided grin a gash of mockery.

'All right,' he gasped, 'I know I can't leave you behind. So I've come. Face to face!'

The air crackled with heat.

As the flames ignited in front of him, he knew it had heard.

Hal stood outside Henllys and watched the smoke rising from the village, listening to Lizzie's footsteps pounding along the grass. He turned to her as she leapt, breathless, down the steps, and she forgot the words she had ready, because she saw he already knew.

'So it's now.' He smiled, wryly. 'Sooner than I'd thought.'

'Hal . . .'

'I'm coming, Lizzie. Nothing will happen to Huw.' As he turned to go with her his eye caught the old grey house, the tall windows warm with sunlight.

'Can you see anyone?' he asked. 'There in the window.'

'Only our reflections.'

He nodded. Then he said, 'I suppose that's what we're really afraid of, isn't it.'

'I don't know.' Confused, she said, 'There's no time, Hal . . .'

He glanced at her, sidelong. 'That's just it. There's no time. Here, there never has been.'

Phil struggled up through the bracken, wiping his sleeve over his face. The vicar slid anxiously behind. 'This isn't the way, Phil. We're no nearer.'

'I can't understand it!' Phil stared furiously around. 'I've been up this path hundreds of times!'

'The smoke's confusing you.' Mitchel swung round, watching the smouldering bracken. Flame spouted below them, and then to the left, roaring across the slope like a hoarse, unnatural breath.

'Get to the top! Quickly!' The vicar's hair was dark with sweat; his shirt stuck to his back. As he scrambled desperately up a cloud of midges rose about him. 'I should have talked to Huw,' he muttered, swiping at them viciously.

'Hal asked me to. God knows what the boy might do.'

'What?' Phil yelled back.

'Nothing!' Nothing. He fell and picked himself up, knowing he should have understood, should have helped, have seen! And yet he had seen. Everything and nothing.

Another yell from Phil made him glance up.

From the summit of the hill a thin blue column of smoke spiralled into the sky.

Huw watched the flames. They roared and raged in front of him. He knew this was the time to act, to do something, but he couldn't make himself move.

Behind the fire the eyes of the stone head taunted him, and even now he didn't know if they had any life or not, or whether it was him, his own fear and grief that was staring back at him. His anger tightened; he gripped his fists and stepped forward.

'Stand still, Huw.'

The voice was to the left, familiar. He glanced over; saw Hal emerge from the trees, and Lizzie behind him, holding the spaniel tight in her arms.

'Don't move.' Hal came through the smoke. 'This is my place, not yours.'

With an effort Huw said, 'It's brought me here. It's haunting me. The fire . . . don't you see, the fire is all my fault.'

'No it's not.' Hal sounded tense, alert. 'And it doesn't want you.'

162

He came up to Huw and faced him, Lizzie watching them both in bewilderment. Ash drifted on them like fine rain. Behind her, Phil and the vicar raced up through the tangled trees.

'The fire's spreading,' Mitchel yelled. 'Hal get him down from here!'

Hal didn't look at him. 'You'll have to do that, John.'

The vicar pushed through the bracken and stopped. Soot smears darkened his face; he shook his head hopelessly.

'I don't understand!'

'Yes you do.' Hal gave him a quick, sharp glance.

'What are you going to do?' Alarmed, Mitchel scrambled up the slope.

'Stay back,' Huw stormed, desperately. 'Can't you see it?'

He glared at the stone head; it stared back, ominous.

'He can't,' Hal said gently. 'None of them can but me.'

'I'm afraid, Hal. I've always been afraid.' Huw twisted his hands together.

'You were an accident,' Hal stared into the sheet of flame, at the hissing, blackening bracken. 'What haunted you was your own fear, of your past, of what happened in the tunnel. You got mixed up with this. But this has been here a long time. You didn't start it. In the hill, in the valley, an ancient hunger. It gave Rowena power. In return she promised it a life.'

'I thought –'

'No.' Hal glanced at him, a bright, strange look. 'No matter how long the tunnel, Huw, there's always the same thing at the end.'

For a moment they were silent, the fire hissing towards them. To Lizzie that second of tension was etched with mystery, as if an invisible host of people watched, among the gnarled trees.

Then Huw jerked back. Hal grabbed his arm, the flame roared and swept up, and at once everything was moving, rushing together, trees and sky and running feet, the whole world collapsing into shadow and flames and the endless, endless scream of brakes. Huw was dragged backwards into a flash of red light and pain, an eruption of shouting, garbled and distorted, and above all one cry, high and harsh and satisfied, that rumbled and crashed down an endless tunnel in his head, and he fell after it, deeper and deeper, into the dark.

CHAPTER 21

With a crash, the sunlight and the street came back. The pavement beneath him was hard and hot; he tried to sit up, sick and shaken. A hand was gripping him; vaguely he struggled against it. All about him the air rang with a great roaring; car-horns, shouts, running feet.

Phil's voice spoke sharply behind his ear. 'Huw! Don't move! Keep still!'

Dizzy, he looked around.

Lizzie was there, holding a black dog. A man was lying in the road with people bending over him. He was a dark-haired man in a white shirt, and as he lay so still on the hot tarmac a trickle of blood ran slowly down his cheek.

'Who is he?' Huw whispered.

'His name's Vaughn. He lived here.'

Huw closed his eyes. He felt puzzled; some memory that he wanted to grip hold of was sliding to the back of his mind; already it was gone, as if it had slipped down a hole and been lost in the dark. But the darkness was quiet, and strangely empty.

Rain fell through it, warm rain, splattering the dust on the ambulance, and the church, and the busy street.

He sat up, stiffly, and licked it from his lips.

CATHERINE FISHER

Darkhenge

'Chloe?' he whispered.
The girl looked back. Her face was shadowed
by great trees, their branches so low she had to duck
under them. The sun shafted through forest. He was sure.
A narrow face, a smile like hers, not seen for
three months. An impudent, spiteful smile.
And a voice. It said, 'Hi, Robbie.'

Rob's sister Chloe lies in a coma after a riding accident,
trapped in a forest of dreams between life and death.
But when a dark druid shape-shifts his way into Rob's
life, despair turns to hope. Because the druid knows
the way through the Unworld, where he claims Chloe
is imprisoned. Could the ominous black ring of timbers
slowly emerging from a secret archaeological dig
hold the key to rescuing her?

BODLEY HEAD
0 370 32859 0

C⊕RBENIC

CATHERINE FISHER

Cal has struggled to cope with his mother's drinking and psychotic episodes since he was six; so when he finally leaves home to live with his uncle he is ruthless about breaking with the past, despite his mother's despair. But getting off the train at the wrong station, Cal finds himself at the mysterious castle of the Fisher King; and the night he spends there plunges him into a wasteland of desolation and adventure as he begins his predetermined quest back to all he has betrayed.

In this intriguing reworking of the Grail Legend, the award-winning author Catherine Fisher has created a gripping novel that moves between myth and a contemporary journey of self-knowledge until one becomes indistinguishable from the other.

'An elaborate and intricate reworking of the Grail Legend...an absorbing story' *BOOKSELLER*

Shortlisted for the Tir Na nOg Prize

DEFINITIONS
0 09 943848 8

CATHERINE FISHER

THE SNOW-WALKER TRILOGY

From the swirling mists and icy realms beyond the edge
of the world came the Snow-walker Gudrun – to rule the
Jarl's people with fear and sorcery. No sword is a match
for her rune-magic and it seems the land may never be
free from her tyranny. But there is a small band of outlaws
determined to defeat Gudrun and restore the rightful Jarl.
This trilogy follows their quest from the first terrifying
journey to meet the mysterious Snow-walker's son, to the
final battle in the land of the soul thieves.

This book includes:

The Snow-walker's Son
The Empty Hand
The Soul Thieves

'A spell-binding story, sure to kindle the imagination'
TES

'An outstanding piece of fiction'
NEW STATESMAN

RED FOX
0 099 44806 8